Sutak

Nadi Palshikar

ALCHEMY

First Impression in 2014

ALCHEMY PUBLISHERS
4767/23, Pratap Street, Darya Ganj,
New Delhi: 110 002

is a registered trademark of Mehras
and is licensed for use to Alchemy Publishers.

Distributed by
MEHRAS BOOKS PVT. LTD.
38 A, Akshoy Kumar Dutta Sarani,
Second Floor, Kolkata-700 006

4767/23, Pratap Street, Darya Ganj, Ansari Road, New Delhi: 110 002

ISBN: 978-81-927491-4-3

Cover design by Manoj Nath

Acknowledgement

A very famous, successful writer read a story sent by an unknown writer. The gorgeous Ms. Shobhaa De. One gracious comment from her and I thought, yes, the book should go out.

Sumana Roy, sent my manuscript to a literary agent. "Read it as you would read my work." She wrote to him. Sumana and I have only exchanged posts and comments online. I hope to meet her someday, to ask her why she is such a kind and warm person.

Like her, there are many online friends whose work I learn so much from, who have added so much to my life. Your encouraging comments to my little stories and posts have kept me going.

Coming back to the book's journey. The very next day, the agent called. Enthusiastic, efficient, energetic Kanishka Gupta of the Writer's Side Literary Agency. Thank you, Kanishka.

The book found a nurturing home at Alchemy Publishers. I am grateful to the entire team.

Manoj Nath wrote a concept note for each of the 'sample' covers he sent. I was moved by the way he had tried to understand the story, the characters. Thank you, Manoj.

Many thanks to Ms. Madhupana Banerjee, for the succinct, valuable editing suggestions. Thanks to Shinjini Mukhopadhyay, editor at Alchemy Publishers.

Rajrupa Das manages writer's anxiety attacks, plans and schedules everything. She also edits. She has, with her excellent editing skills contributed so much. Thank you, Rajrupa.

Sona Agrawal, gentle, reassuring angel to the book. "Do not hesitate to ask me if you have any other doubt." She always wrote in her instant, helpful, encouraging email replies. Thank you for everything, Sona.

Were it not for all of you, this book would not exist.

Similarly, I owe my writer existence to the following people.

Students of Mass Communication at Symbiosis where I was visiting faculty, I learnt so much from all of you.

FTII people- teachers and students, past and present, and of all streams, thank you.

The 2006-2007 batch of the FTII Screenplay Writing course, you know how special you are and how proud I am of you.

Classmates of the first batch (2004-2005) of the FTII Screenplay writing course, thank you for that magical year.

Thanks to Mr. Ashwini Malik who was professor, coordinator and friend to all of us that year.

That first dozen, now with all the subsequent batches form a closely knit group.

Finally, Mr. Anjum Rajabali. I was a student in Sir's class ten years ago.

Home-

I am blessed to have my mother Dr. Saroj Lokgariwar, my beloved sister Chicu Lokgariwar and brother-in-law Keith Goyden as family.

The extremely intelligent and beautiful Mukta Palshikar is my most cherished person.

Lastly and above all, my one sustenance-

Thank you Girish Palshikar, for our 'wrong-recipe' *Khichdi;* for everything that you put into it.

Nadi Palshikar

A woman is buying panties. She is 34 years old, flustered, beautiful. She is dressed for obscurity.

She points to a pack on the shelf. The salesperson gets it down. The woman stops her from opening the packet.

'I want them in all six colours,' she says.

An unusually large number of rather sensible, ordinary underwear is stuffed into a shopping bag, for she has chosen all six colours, all three flowery patterns of three other kinds – all in one size larger than what she needs.

Many loose, cotton panties – she looks at them as if she anticipates more than just comfort.

Then, Lalita looks shyly at the sexy lingerie displayed in the windows. The two salespersons look at each other and giggle.

She is scandalized by the little bikini pants, especially the pink ones, they think. She has never worn pink bikini pants, they are sure.

They are wrong; she just never buys them.

***

She has been buying undergarments from Embroidery House for years now. They have seen her through maternity gowns, nappies for her baby, bloomers for her little girl, and for her own once in three months shopping.

A good customer, Mr. Meghani, the owner knows her as, who buys a good quantity, never anything expensive or fancy, but regular. She is appreciative of classy stuff; she was the first one to congratulate him when they started stocking the new expensive foreign brands.

When it comes to herself, however, there seems to be no regard to sensuousness or even variety in her ridiculously 'wholesale' kind of buying, he has often seen the staff joking about the number of panties she buys.

Many panties and nothing else.

Hers is not a body that needs any of the girdles that Embroidery House specialises in, she has always been thin. A little too thin, he has heard the salesgirls tell her about padded bras but she has always stuck to a local brand of sports bra which further flattens her chest.

Well, he thinks, each to her own. He has seen too many idiosyncrasies to be surprised by anything now. Usually, he can tell a lot about a woman, her job, even the stage her marriage is going through by the underwear she buys.

This lady is something of an enigma however, one of those rare mysteries that still keep the shop day interesting.

He smiles as he gives back her change.

'I will take them to the car for you.'

Mr. Meghani is surprised to see his son open the door for her himself. An MBA from one of those new management colleges that have sprung all over town, the boy had always said he would not waste his time selling underwear. After trying that 'something better' for a year, he has now started helping with the shop.

Now, as he sees his son behave with this uncharacteristic politeness, he smiles to himself on seeing the disappointment on Mr. MBA's face at his offer being refused.

Mr. and Mrs. Meghani will finally be able to retire to growing strawberries at Mahabaleshwar soon; their son has noticed the mystery that some women have, and now, working at Embroidery House will never lose its charm.

***

Why is it called Embroidery House, she wonders as she steps out of the shop, there is not a single embroidered item for sale!

There are bras.

Trainer bras for little girls.

Cute trainer bras.

What about those girls who, unlike their friends, have no breasts yet?

Sexy bras for the new brides. Available up to a certain size only.

Only up to a certain size, for surely fat girls didn't dream of looking sexy on their wedding night !

Sports bras to make a girl look sporty even if she is not.

Padded bras for those who think their breasts are not womanly enough.

And finally, at the other extreme end from the bras for cute teenagers, are the bras for the woman who has undergone a mastectomy.

Breasts that once needed support or padding.

Breasts that were once either too small or too big.

Breasts that once needed lace; otherwise how would her man know they were sensuous?

Breasts that were finally cut away.

Bras for breasts at different stages in a woman's life.

Then, bras for breasts that no longer exist.

So many bras.

So many slips, half slips, skirt slips, corsets.

Not a single thread of embroidery on any of them.

Maybe, embroidered clothes were sold here once, clean white handkerchiefs and undergarments made pretty by the needlework of some woman.

Maybe, the family that owned this shop had owned another in Sind, and although this post-partition shop had had to adapt itself to the market, or maybe that embroiderer woman was dead, or too hurt or old to embroider, and the younger generation of women had made new careers, new lives in this new land, so there was no embroidery to sell, but the name had stuck, as names from the past tend to, even if nothing else is really the same.

***

Akka means older sister. As a baby, Vinodini had shortened it to *Akku*. She had called out this name which she made up herself, out of love. Then Mother began to call her by that name so that Vinodini wouldn't call her older sister by her first name, that would be disrespectful; and slowly, everybody called her *Akku*, and the name stuck — this name which meant she was somebody's older sister, but herself not big enough to deserve the original, the more formal *Akka*.

'Akku,' Vinodini had called out once and had run across the road. Reaching safely to the other side, she was delighted at having scared her older sister who had stood beyond the stream of passing cars, terrified.

Lalita stands on the road divider with bags containing vegetables and groceries.

Should she cross back to the *nariyal paani* stall, she is thirsty, or should she cross over to the other side? She is tired, a nap maybe, before her daughter comes home. She is tired, but happy at the thought of cooking the tofu that she has bought; her daughter likes it very much.

Shopping gives housewives a false sense of providing for their family without really having to earn. She finds herself thinking what Vinodini would have said.

She realises that the others must have heard her muttering to herself, for a small group of people waits with her to cross the road. This is not the same group that stood with her when she first reached here. Every few moments a small group gathers. Two such groups cross the road. She is not able to. The vehicles are too many, too fast for her. She stands there.

Then, as if at the worst possible moment, she rushes across confused, afraid, dodging vehicles. Clothes, hair in complete disarray.

***

Lalita pushes back her hair with the back of her hand. She vigorously beats rice flour in a big vessel. She likes the feel of the wet, coarse dough on her hands.

And the rhythm.

Professor Jean-Claude Kaufman tells us that housework is a deeply sensual experience. Faking in bed has clearly not been enough. They have to fake arousal even while cleaning the fridge. Vinodini quoting from Germaine Greer's work, as and when it suited her; in a way that suited her, often out of context. She has developed this habit of mouthing lines from books in that world she inhabits — a world where not many are likely to have read Greer.

Lalita can imitate her sister's voice aloud now. Nobody can hear her.

Alone, in an ultra-modern kitchen, complete with a new-fangled chimney, futuristic-looking shelves and the latest microwave oven, Lalita beats rice flour with her bare hands.

She makes idlis from scratch, the way her grandmother had done; she does it because her mother had never made them.

Her hair is like her mother's, everybody says. She still does her hair like her mother would tell the maid to do it — tame the curls, and tie it in a tight oily plait. Now she turns the plait in circles to make a tight bun at the base of her head. Like her grandmother, she pins a *gajra* of white flowers around it.

The smell of the *mogra* flowers will help her let her mind wander away to a remembered garden, away from the party tonight.

***

Mahesh gets dressed for a formal occasion. Mahesh gets dressed that is, he is always dressed for a formal occasion, Lalita thinks, and wonders whether it is not his attire but the occasions themselves, for it is only formal occasions that Lalita and he go dressed up to.

It does not occur to her that it is not the clothes, not the outing but that she associates the word 'formal' with their time together, because of her behaviour whenever she is around him.

She is formal, suitable; she is as is required of her.

She tries to be.

Mahesh is looking for the right tie in the wardrobe that they share. While searching for his tie, he selects a heavy traditional saree and flings it on the bed.

He is dressing up to show-off, and he would like her to be dressed up to be shown-off.

She is as is required of her.

She tries to be.

Almost always.

Not tonight.

Ironically, the bigger the party, the easier it is to

disobey dressing rules. There will be so many others obeying them, categorising themselves. There will be the wives of successful male doctors, good bodies with more time to maintain figures and keep up to date about the current fashions.

The successful women doctors do not have that much time, but they have more money, so their clothes are more expensive; also, they will make an effort to be 'understated', subtle to set themselves apart from the 'wives'.

Years ago, doctor's parties were a showcase of rich silk sarees. Hardly anyone in Pune wears those any more. 'Anyone', 'everyone' to Lalita, means the medical fraternity in Pune; they are the only people she meets.

Will meeting different people make the bearing of the present social circle easier, or will it simply mean more people that must be talked to, smiled at, faced?

She smiles as she recollects an oft-repeated suggestion made to people with stage fright — imagine the audience is naked.

She does not want to think about the people she is about to face, it is easier for her to think about clothes.

What had she been thinking about? Yes, western clothes. 'Western' the signs on the trouser racks in malls proclaim. Why? Chinese women wear trousers, in the movies at least. But then, the women in the old

black and white Indian movies, the really old ones that
Lalita likes to watch, wear sarees.

Sarees. Yes, there will be the wives of the senior most
doctors still wearing sarees, their hips too settled to be
gymmed into trousers, but other than them, everyone
seems to have adopted western clothes. Mornings see
'ethnic' kurtas teamed with jeans, salwaars are passé.
Evening wear comes from racks called just that —
evening wear. It is not western, it has sequins and a
smaller version of a dupatta; it is not Indian, for the
salwaar has been replaced by a pair of trousers made
from material which was not meant for trousers.

Whatever it is, there are only so many racks and as
a result, everybody, Lalita thinks sometimes, looks the
same.

But tonight, there will be designer western tops and
nicely cut trousers. Mahesh is now at the very top, they
need not socialise with anyone but the 'number ones'
in every speciality.

Mahesh has only just made it to this top thing,
whatever it is; they are not yet one of the important
people.

Everybody else will seem to have known each other
forever. Every woman will have acquired that poise,
that attractiveness that only success can bring.

Lalita cannot and need not even try to blend in.

She can wear anything she wants.

The difference between her and the others can be.

In their eyes, Lalita is an ordinary woman.

So ordinary that they won't notice how she stands out.

***

'I'm waiting outside.' It is what Mahesh thinks is his polite way of telling her to hurry the hell up. He has already put on his cheerful life-of-the-party voice.

He is waiting to go to a room full of people who will admire him, there will be some who think he is a bit of a show-off; and there will be Lalita watching all this, worrying about him, wondering whether this exhibitionism is a disguise her husband puts on.

She will see him — a scared little boy at a fancy dress party dressed up as a brave warrior.

A child whose greatest sorrow is her looks, over-dressed as a princess.

A shorthaired girl weighed down by her Rapunzel wig.

She will want to see him as vulnerable because she wants to love him.

'I am waiting outside.'

She does not answer, and quickly chooses the comfort of a simple cotton salwaar kurta, this party will go on for too long and it is a hot night.

***

Raga *Basant* evokes the summer, a forgotten summer.

A non-air-conditioned, real summer from the past.

Her hosts, a cultured couple, connoisseurs of Hindustaani classical music have naturally chosen to play it on their expensive CD player.

They are knowledgeable about the music, but obviously do not love it enough to not drown it in conversations and sounds of feigned delight at seeing each other.

Her favourite singer's voice fights the noise to call out to her as soon as she reaches the door, but she cannot respond , instead, she acknowledges the 'How are you, Lalita?' that is given to her with the speed at which one would hand one's railway ticket to the ticket checker even as one is walking hurriedly towards the taxi stand.

Walking away, as the hostess is already, with what she has borrowed from Lalita in exchange for that token question.

Mahesh is led away; she can hardly spot him in the crowd. The crowd will soon start admiring him, flattering him even. Even encouraging his only partly joking statements like what he's saying right now — 'Two psychosomatic MI admissions today. Life is good.'

What had driven those two people into believing that they were about to die, had they wanted to die?

Were their near and dear ones worried that they might have had a Myocardial Infarction, a heart attack, or were they disappointed when it turned out to be a false alarm?

The others laugh along with Dr. Mahesh Gune. Some nervously, they are good men, good doctors. Some heartily, they enjoy the joke, that does not mean that they are bad people, that they are callous, that they will do that which is not in the best interest of their patients. They are very good at their work, Lalita knows this for a fact — they save lives.

What bothers her is that this kind of a joke is allowed in a group of people practising the noblest of all professions.

Noble profession indeed, it is all very well for Lalita to talk about Medicine with an exaggerated reverence, Mahesh says, she, after all, does not practise it.

***

To practise Medicine was all her Father had wanted to do. That he did it so well, that he wanted it so much, was responsible for his having to give it up.

The cottage hospital at Wadi was a neglected, defunct place when he got himself posted there. A Master's degree in Surgery from Mumbai, new ideas, idealisms of a young man who wanted to 'Do something'. And, he did.

Dr. Indrajeet Patwardhan's hard work woke the staff

up to work. After the initial resistance to his strict ways, the nurses, ward attendants and sweepers began to like being regular, diligent for this man, and slowly began to feel proud of their work, their cottage hospital.

The referral centres at Goa got a respite from patients flocking from Wadi as most surgeries were done at the cottage hospital now. *The Indian Journal of Surgery* published case reports and papers by this young doctor.

All this was good, and then the gastroenteritis epidemic started.

The hospital staff chose that very day to go on strike to protest against the Pawar Sister incident.

Dr. Patwardhan had suspended a staff nurse called Pratibha Pawar from work. She had asked for money to attend to a poor woman in labour. A month had passed since and Pawar Sister was even back to her duties when the gastroenteritis epidemic broke out and the staff union decided to protest.

Patients poured in, but there was no staff. It took Dr. Patwardhan half an hour to organise volunteers. He had repaired a leg broken in a motorcycle accident, and that patient, still limping but strong had turned up with fifty of his college friends.

Inspired by the doctor who himself did not return home that fortnight, the epidemic was brought under control.

The staff, who would be loyal to this man one day, who would respect him, stood and watched.

There were some other people who watched: they saw how this man could mobilise people, they had already known of the name the villagers had given him – *Dev Manus*. A God-like person.

Simple, honest people, they were not shy to really call him that; but then, don't we all look for a God?

There are some other people though, who are always on the lookout for someone revered.

To find a God, and then, to use him.

Three months later some people from the ruling party had convinced Lalita's father that he would be able to serve the people he had come to love better if he became a member and even insisted that he accept their party's candidature for the upcoming assembly elections, which he won.

Dr. Patwardhan continued to practise Medicine however, politics couldn't keep him away from the work which was his life.

It took death to do that.

It would be impossible to survive in a world replete with pain and death, Mahesh likes to say, if one was not to allow oneself a little bit of a light-hearted attitude. She catches his eye now; she knows that he can see what he calls her disapproving look. *You have absolutely no sense of humour Lalita*, he will say tonight.

That may start the usual complaints about how dull she is, how incapable of enjoying anything. Or, he might say the same thing about her having no sense of humour, but turn it into an affectionate comment; he might even put his arm around her in the car. He will feel romantic towards his wife if he has had a stimulating conversation with a woman at the party, a woman with a sense of humour, a woman who is not dull like his wife.

So much of a man's post-party behaviour depends on the kind of conversation he has had with a woman.

Considering that it is such an important factor, little effort seems to go into making it possible, Lalita thinks, as she sees how yet again, the men are talking only to each other, the women stand apart.

Usually, it is one of the older women, one of the older 'wives', who is called Madam or *Bhabhiji'* by most of the men in the group, she is not just a woman beginning to converse with a man, she will go across to where they are standing and ask whether the shop-talk is over, say that the women are bored, why aren't the men talking to them, she might even pat a younger doctor on his back.

No, this is not the eighteenth century, not some village gathering, this is a party populated by people who are successful, interesting even, at least to each other and the segregation will end, there will be groups, one-to-one conversations, even flirtations, but it will have to be initiated by that older woman. Where is she, who will be that woman tonight, Lalita wonders why such a move has not been made yet.

***

'It's the way she moves, she looks just about okay I guess, it's the way she moves that irritates me.' someone says.

They are all feeling so low, Lalita can spot the signs. This talking about a person instead of thoughts or at least feelings, and if not those then current affairs! That too, a person from their immediate surroundings, it is clear to Lalita now, this is going to be one of those parties from which Lalita will return home feeling that her life is stuck in trivialities, that she is trivial.

They are talking about a new cardiologist who has just joined a leading hospital in town after working in the UK for ten years.

She is still single, they have found out. Thirty-five and not married, giving time to her career, developing herself instead of 'settling down'.

'Still' single, that's what they say about Vinodini.

She is smart, fit and confident; they have compared her to themselves.

Vinodini compares her fit body to Lalita's unfit thinness often, pushing her sister to join a gym, Lalita likes these discussions, she takes care not to look too fondly at her sister, proudly flexing her muscles like a little boy. 'Feel my biceps.'

Vinodini does not like what she calls Lalita's 'Mamma eyes'.

Keeping an eye on her sister all the time — that's what Lalita does, Vinodini says.

***

Last week her voice sounded as if she had a slight cold. Check your temperature, Lalita had said.

She had not been surprised that there was no thermometer in that independent pad.

She was hurt that there was nobody to look after Vinodini when she had a cold.

How can her own hand know whether her forehead is hot, the hand too is part of the suffering body.

Her sister's body – coveted, made love to, enjoyed.

But when this body was ill, it was alone.

So many lovers.

Not one hand to touch her forehead and see whether she had fever.

***

Lalita does not offer to go over and take care of her. Vinodini feels stifled if she finds her sister attached to her.

Free, unattached the women are saying, perhaps with a touch of envy, Lalita smiles to herself.

They are so engrossed in their dissection of the new cardiologist on their scene.

'Why are you smiling Mrs. Gune?' one of them asks Lalita.

'She is exactly the kind we should be wary of!'

We the wives should be wary always of everybody that our husbands might find attractive.

We the wives should be vigilant, lest we lose our title of wife.

The more they gossip about this cardiologist, the more she reminds Lalita of Vinodini.

The 'we' that Lalita is seen as a part of have to guard themselves against threats like this woman who she can see is so much like Vinodini.

What did Lalita and Vinodini see each other as?

Lalita sees her reflection in the glass of the window.

***

Her hostess passes by, she smells even more strongly of perfume now, she's just back from her bedroom, having freshened up, as she makes a point of telling everybody.

Everybody knows that she smokes secretly, only confirmed by the over-compensatory perfume.

The party must be stressful for her, she needed to smoke. How must her life be that she had to sneak away to do it? Lalita feels like talking to her, maybe she could answer that question she had been asked before Mahesh was whisked away, which had left no time for the answer to be heard, even spoken.

I am fine she starts to say, but her hostess has been called away; thankfully, how would that have sounded? I am fine. Is she?

She looks at her reflection in the window and runs her right hand along the *kurta* neckline to confirm that her bra strap is well hidden.

Unsure of her appearance, insecure about Mahesh-looking totally out of place.

***

Vinodini is unsure about her looks.

She grimaces at the bathroom mirror and looks for imaginary wrinkles on her neck and face.

She makes a funny face. She is obviously caricaturing Lalita's mannerisms and lip movements.

Her sister's voice.

'There is so much love inside you...'

'...a man who will look after you *beta*.'

Beta? Yes, she is eight years younger, but not her child for crying out aloud!

Anything but that '*beta*'!

'Come, sit by me, sweetie,' he calls her to the bedroom.

'Sit by' him? Who was he kidding? They hadn't driven home from the meeting straight to her apartment, his of course had his wife and kids in it, hers was convenient, to 'sit by' each other.

He wanted to have sex, and it was not only her apartment that was so convenient; she has increasingly begun to feel that she is nothing but a convenience in his full, successful great life. Hers, on the other hand, is beginning to feel increasingly empty. But at least the evening will be filled by something. What?

'Coming,' she says, just that — 'coming'; she cannot think of an endearment to answer to the 'sweetie'.

Her married lover calls out an endearment.

Does he hear his wife saying 'You don't you call me honey any more'? Vinodini wonders.

Her married lover, as if determined that he is not going to rush things, is deliberate in his foreplay.

Like the kissing, murmuring of endearments that is going on now as if there is another woman in the room, instructing him to do the correct thing, to at least get it right with this other woman.

His nose tickles her thigh and she suppresses a giggle, she looks as if she is winking at his wife who stands in the room, directing the proceedings, so to speak.

His illicit lover is sharing a joke with his wife.

Vinodini wonders why if he knows the routine, so to speak, does he not do it with his wife, for all this *is* the wife's routine.

The way he goes through it systematically, she can feel in her skin that it is what the wife has said she wants.

She must have listed the things that he did not do, how he did not care about her pleasure.

Why then, doesn't he, now that he has learnt, give all this to her, and save their marriage?

So that Vinodini can be spared of the blame for breaking it?

But by the time the stage of personal insults has been reached, by the time the wife gives up trying to protect his feelings and the screams have started, calling him a graceless lover, an impotent fool, other things have gone wrong too.

Marriages are like that, by the time an intimate fault is vocalised, it is not simply a matter of correcting it; it has been vocalised because something else is beyond repair.

There is, for him, a feeling so tender that at this particular moment she wouldn't be lying if she whispered those three words in his ear.

She knows it makes him happy, even though he knows that he does not really want what it implies and that Vinodini does not want 'emotional complications', to hear her say those three words especially just as he is, as he is just about to now empty himself inside her. Vinodini knows and does not say anything.

Empty himself inside her.

Vinodini realises that she was not hoping that the evening will be filled by something, but that it will help her empty herself of something.

Just before she came to him, she had been imitating her sister, making fun of her. This imitating had been okay when it was fun; nowadays, it gets her into a strange mood. She needs to clear her mind of something, she does not know what.

Their nights, once a month and a weekend at the annual conference are just that: a time where she empties herself.

Is that what men mean when they say I'll fuck you senseless?

Is that what men realise?

That they are just something that helps a woman forget, for a while. Forget what?

And what was she doing, pontificating about married men and extra-marital affairs, when this married man was giving, at least trying to give her pleasure.

Enjoy girl, she tells herself. Sex, sex albeit without even a pretence of love is certainly better than late night TV!

He looks at her face – has he been okay, he probably wonders, or is he losing his touch?

Always, there is something different to please her, in gratitude for having a younger smart woman in bed; something exciting.

Marital sex must have a higher degree of comfort, she thinks; none of this 'at your exciting best' and no changing hotels, making excuses for just one day a month of sex.

Regular albeit boring sex is one underrated benefit of marriage, Vinodini sees her face in the mirror. She insists on all lamps in the bedroom being switched off, the only light is that coming through the open door.

***

Lalita's face, lit only by a dim night lamp. Mahesh is asleep. It is obvious that they have been making love.

She wants the bruise on her thigh to be covered.

Why is so much emphasis placed on undressing?

To cover a loved body is love.

If someone could dress this bruise, she would feel love.

Lalita pulls on a slip. The lacy material irritates her, she thinks of the softness of the plain cotton in Embroidery House, and steps off the bed.

Her foot falls on an open magazine. A picture of a model in bikini pants and a fur stole around her body.

They have forgotten to draw a bruise on her thigh for is it really Lalita's bruise or was it meant for the girl in this picture?

The beginning of hardness around the model's mouth, the hardness that creeps in when you are dressed to pretend you are someone else.

Women whose partners look at these pictures can only feel an empathy for these models, for what was the difference between braiding your hair for the school-girl look and at the same time showing your breasts to turn people on, and wearing a traditional saree for a good-housewife look and also trying to talk intelligently, so that people don't look down upon you for being 'just a' housewife?

Does she think that women do it because they want to, when Vinodini quotes things like *'The wife is eager to enter into his fantasies and to impersonate the various female figures that turn him on.'* Would she say that if she knew that her sister was such a Wife?

Lalita chews on the lace of her slip nervously. She pulls up her foot.

Lalita is ten years old. Her frock collar in her mouth, eyes closed precariously, she sits on the edge of her table. She bends down and looks under.

Slowly, she starts to put a leg down. A tomcat purrs.

The sounds of two cats fighting.

The child holds her throat.

She gags on the water that she is pushing as deep into her throat as possible. Lalita adds some dettol to a mug of water and gurgles.

Water clears taste, erases the distaste.

Water cleans everything. She will go for a swim tomorrow.

***

Aphra is a dark, strong ten-year old. She is poised on a high diving board. She looks at her mother who is in the water. Lalita indicates that she should dive. Aphra dives gracefully and swims to her mother. Lalita smiles proudly.

Aphra presses her mother's shoulders down playfully. It is her turn now. Lalita rests her elbows on the edge. She looks at the crowds around the pool.

A young man shows off to a girl. A handsome husband teaches his wife to float. A portly man doing 'warm up exercises' smiles at her.

Children dressed in white martial arts clothes run around the pool. The karate teacher keeps time.

He holds a little girl's elbows and straightens her arms.

Lalita's elbow suddenly slips of the edge. She sputters for a moment.

Lalita swims away.

Lalita leans against the wall and looks towards Vinodini. Audrey's daughters swim away. Aphra has a wry expression on her face.

Lalita swims very fast towards Aphra. Her head emerges. Aphra looks at her mother quizzically. Aphra looks behind her at Audrey who's finishing a sentence, parts of which Lalita has not heard as she was swimming.

'Your plans about adopting a baby sister for this one...'

Aphra hoists herself out of the pool and says with that wry expression of hers.

'A baby sister! That would be great! Just like Mum and Vinu *Mavshi,*' and swims away.

Lalita is about to follow her, when Audrey gestures that they swim laps together. Lalita is clearly the more confident, more graceful swimmer. Audrey is breathless. 'What happens to this confidence when you are out on land, mermaid?' she pants as she goes to the ladder, perches on a rung, and looks at Lalita as she pushes a stray curl back into her cap, and disappears.

Lalita swims very slowly under water.

Gleaming blue tiles.

Clear water all around her.

Her head emerges for a moment; and then, she dives down.

A crack in the floor of the pool.

She touches it.

Lalita holds a stone at the bottom of a lake. There are plants growing inside. Lalita's feet touch the muddy, stone-filled bottom of the lake.

Her face is beautiful in the sunlight streaming through the water.

Sunlight mellowing itself for the creatures that stay under water, creatures that cannot take the brightness of the world above.

Here, in the swimming pool there is only an electric bulb. Lalita tries to cut off the light by placing her hands over the lamp. The glare disturbs her. She closes her eyes.

Eyes closed, Aphra's Grandmother does not look up even when Aphra calls out to her to show off her backstroke. She should go and wake her up, Lalita decides and goes off to get some space to change alone without her friend and their daughters.

***

A woman should finish her childbearing by the age of thirty indeed, is it any of this doctor's business. Vinodini of course does not say this aloud and puts her feet in the stirrups, why doesn't she just insert the Multiload, so that Vinodini can go back to her work?

But a coffee first, she will tell Nikhil who has told her that he will stall the car right outside the clinic, even drive around a bit if a traffic cop spots him, instead of finding a parking space. Nikhil will buy her a cup of coffee and as she drinks it, he will look at her as if she has had a major surgery. Funny, dear Nikhil! She is relieved at the thought that he is waiting for her outside as the IUCD insertion has made her a little dizzy. These dizzy spells and the increased bleeding, especially on the second day of her periods, she has forgotten to tell the doctor about them, but she pays the receptionist and walks out of the clinic anyway, there is too much work at the office.

But first, there is Nikhil. How has he managed it, he hates to look for parking; but there he is with a closed paper glass of coffee, how did he know she wanted some?

Another one of *those* thoughts to be pushed away, or made into something funny before they decide to stay.

Convert this into something trite; perhaps 'tea telepathy', or 'coffee connection', and use it in their new campaign. She hopes he will start talking about work right way, she does not want any awkward questions about how it went, and so on, and Nikhil does talk of work right away. He has sent her a link to some article he liked in some advertising online magazine, has she seen it, he asks.

***

'You used to read old magazines in the attic.' Mother reminds Lalita, Lalita does not remind her why she used to run away to the attic at all.

The topic of magazines has come up because Mother has been reading the same magazine she was reading yesterday and has forgotten that she has already shown Lalita the recipe she is showing her now. Vinodini likes it, she says and tells her how as a child Vinodini never liked *karelas* and then one day the servant cooked them this way and then ... she goes on. Lalita has heard this story before. She remembers when Vinodini started liking *karela,* and of course, Mother remembers it. Everything that Vinodini ate or did not eat, at that age is of great significance; what surprises her is that Mother remembers all this in such detail, but has forgotten that she has told this story just yesterday, she has forgotten that she has read this magazine yesterday. She keeps nodding at Mother, tugging at the tablecloth on the antique table as she looks at an old photograph — Nalini and Anuradha Auntie seated on chairs.

Nalini holds Vinodini, who is only two years old, close to her. Lalita, ten years, stands behind and looks at them.

Lalita had looked on in wonder as Mother had spoken to Anuradha Auntie yesterday.

Nalini remembers everything Anuradha had said about her, proving as usual, that Lalita worries unnecessarily, that she imagines problems where there are none. But then, two hours after Anuradha has left, it is Lalita who hears Mother complaining how nobody comes to visit her these days; she has totally forgotten that her friend had come and chatted the whole morning, and that she herself had talked about people, things back home.

Home is the place Mother chose to leave ten years ago, when she bought a flat for herself.

Home is the place she left when she could finally stop pretending to think of it as home.

Home is the house she hated.

The house that Vinodini wants to sell now.

***

Every time Vinodini returns from one of her road trips to Goa, she tells Lalita about it. How Lalita should not sigh in one of her happily-ever-after hopes about the man who has accompanied Vinodini on her trip.

'I will stop telling you if you behave like this,' she warns her older sister, and goes on to say what fun it was, how having this old house in Wadi is an added attraction, how they stopped there, how Radhabai mistook this friend for the one she had taken along last year. She emphasises how she drove for 'exactly half the distance'; Mahesh never lets Lalita drive on highways.

Equality is very important in such matters she says and Lalita fights what Vinodini will call one of her 'sighs'. She tries not to think that for her sister this 'casual' trip is full of attachment, even love. That for the man it is just a trip with an attractive intelligent liberated girl, he will have taken an autorickshaw home as they entered Pune 'because his house is closer from the Satara Road Octroi Naka corner' and Vinodini will have driven to her flat alone; that the joke about Radhabai does not make her laugh because she knows why last year's thing ended.

'Thing is, I can't wait until I inherit it, Akku, we have to sell the house now, what's the use of getting the money years down the line?'

Vinodini decides this each time she stops at the house for a night. The old dark house stands in contrast to the bright successful advertising agency she plans to own.

And what does she mean by waiting to inherit?

Waiting for Mamma to die?

Does Lalita let the thought of Mother's death cross her mind?

Maybe, but she would never wait for something to happen, she has stopped hoping that something that may change her life for the better, will take place, ever.

***

Mother seems better whenever she sees her, Vinodini reminds her sister yet again.

Then why does she not go and live in Vinodini's little apartment when she visits Pune, Lalita feels, why does Vinodini not invite her to do so?

Meeting Mother for a while is nice; putting her up is a nervous, criticism-filled time.

Let alone taking Mother to her place, Vinodini does not even stay in the city the whole week that Mother is here.

Her road trips to Wadi often coincide with Mother's visit to Lalita's house, from where she picks up the key to the old house, takes a friend with her — Mother's not there to ask questions.

She has returned from one of these trips now. And has found time for her 'duty-visit', and can claim how happy Mother seems whenever she visits.

It is the cocoa fruit and the big lemons that you got back from Wadi, Lalita tells her, anything about the old house seems to bring about calm, even coherence.

Lalita cooks in the kitchen. The smell of mushrooms wafts to Mother's room. Mother is in a pleasant mood as she is when Vinodini visits.

Vinodini knows that it is her visit that mellows Mother down, but that Mother will never acknowledge that.

Lalita knows that this is not because she does not want Vinodini to know that she is happy to see her, but because she does not want anyone to know she is happy.

'Mushrooms!' Mother puckers up her nose. 'Doesn't Akku know that I am allergic to them?'

Doesn't Mother know that mushrooms are Vinodini's favourite vegetable? Mother, who remembers about the *karelas*?

Mother chooses to forget this because it is the one favourite dish of Vinodini's that Lalita cooks. Thanks to the allergy.

It is because the smell irritates her, Vinodini assumes that Mother tells her to close the door.

She shuts the door and comes back to pretend to admire the sweater that Mother is knitting for her. Once again, it is for her; Mother never knits for Akku. An affectionate conversation is called for but Mother has put down her knitting and is getting up.

'I'll close the door myself,' she says.

'I have closed it, Mamma.'

'The back door.' Mother mutters and starts putting her feet into her slippers.

'There is no back door, Mamma.' Vinodini says and gently tries to make Mother sit.

'Shut the back door' Mother coughs and starts rocking herself.

This is one of those times that Lalita has to be called in. This is one of those times that Lalita comes to Mother without being called.

Here she is, standing in the doorway, her hand holding the door open.

'This house has no back door, Mamma,' she says simply and returns to the kitchen.

She has not even had to enter the room.

Vinodini is surprised to see that Mother has taken up her knitting again, peering into her pattern book.

The cough has stopped, she is calm and still.

'This house has no back door.'

But hadn't Vinodini said exactly the same thing? With no effect?

Was Mother scared of Lalita?

Lalita's curt, rude manner startles Mother. What Lalita said had calmed her down.

'This house has no back door.'

Hadn't Vinodini said exactly the same thing?

Or had she?

'THIS house has no back door.'

***

We should take Mamma to the old house, Lalita says, surprised at herself, because she has never gone there in ten years. Ten years ago, Mother sold the other place which housed Father's *Jana Sampark Karyalay* to a builder, and bought a modern flat for Vinodini.

The builder has demolished Father's office for a building in its place and to make a lot of profit.

Lalita has not had the courage to visit and see what has come up in place of the office where Father had met the people from his constituency – Our people, he had told her.

Our house, she tries to say the same things to Vinodini, she has said them so many times now. Vinodini talks about selling the house so often these days.

You decide, she tells her younger sister; come and stay with Mamma and me for a few days, and if you feel the same, we will sell the house.

Vinodini protests that she has just returned and that, in fact, whenever she goes there she wants to sell it. Lalita knows that it is because she and Mother are not in the house when Vinodini sees it.

This time, she will drag Mother away from her 'convenient' flat, this time she will take her sister with her.

'Let us go together,' she says and lets her sister decide the dates, depending on when she can take some days off from work.

***

'A week off from the hospital? You don't seem to have an idea of what that means! I have worked my ass off so that you can have this "successful doctor's wife" lifestyle.'

'Who says you haven't, Mahesh? We were planning

that Mauritius trip, we always go for a holiday wherever you decide we should. I am just asking you to use that week of leave to come home with me.'

'Just because you don't have a job, you don't know what it means.' Mahesh sits on a sofa, TV remote in hand, a journal of cardiology lying face down next to him.

The television shows silent images, alternating between a sports and a music channel.

The sound comes on for just enough time to drown her meek 'But when I wanted to take up that medical social worker job… '

And is switched off again for his,

'No wife of mine is going to answer back like that. You want to take up a 5000 bucks-a-month job? And, that too in a hospital where I'm a consultant? I know you want to embarrass me, but please can we leave my workplace out of this?'

Lalita runs her finger along the spines of some neatly arranged books.

'That M.A. was the only time I ever excelled…'

Mahesh turns his face away from the TV to look mockingly at her.

'Middle-class Maharashtrian women studying psychology or taking up social work courses is a sure sign that they are planning to leave their "oppressive and patriarchal husbands",'says he. His artificial cruel laugh scratches.

Lalita looks at her hand. The nail of her pointer finger scratches out the cuticle of her thumb. Her thumb bleeds.

'Generalisations, prejudices — it hurts me to hear you talk like that,' she mutters.

Mahesh, his elbow on the back of the sofa, turns towards her. Then he gets up. Lalita shields her face with her hands. Her palms face him. He has hurt her before. He is glad she knows that it is a possibility.

Lalita puts her hands down. She looks at his almost laughing face. She makes an attempt to look stronger than she is.

To look stronger is necessary to continue this conversation, now that he has brought it up, she herself is never allowed to broach the topic.

'If not in the same hospital, then...'

He realises his mistake. He had brought this up to show her down and now she wants to talk about it.

He dismisses her off by turning his attention to the remote, changes the channel and says,

'Please Lalita! Not that boring old rural hospital threat. One day without the *bais* and the driver and you'd be back in no time.'

The TV noise comes on, louder this time. Lalita feels 'attacked' by the sounds. She stares into space. Her hands are under the table, scratching out more blood from the thumb. Then, she kneels down and opens the left lower cupboard of the table. She opens a book. It opens at a page which has been undone the most number of times — to reveal a small photograph of a bearded doctor with some tribals.

The Raga *Megh* in her head drowns out the sports commentary, the ad jingles, everything but only for a while. She snaps out to look at an ad that is being shown — two sanitary napkins animated to look like shoes walking in puddles, 'soaking' up. Vinodini has thought of this ridiculous idea.

***

'Trust my sister to come up with such a ridiculous idea', Vinodini shouts into Nikhil's ear at a traffic signal. She has lifted up the visor of her helmet. She is scoffing at the idea, laughing at her sister but for some reason, the eyeshade is fogged. She wipes it with her hand.

Mother wipes a fogged glass window. Both are in the backseat of a beautiful black car. Mother has her arm around Vinodini. She points outside the window. It is a bright morning. The road winds along a river. Everything is green and beautiful. Vinodini is trying to see...

The visor snaps shut, she even turns her head away and hopes Nikhil hasn't seen what she wants to avoid. Thankfully her sister hasn't seen her — she thinks as they pass Mahesh's car.

***

Mahesh drives recklessly only when Lalita tells him to drive carefully.

Now, he looks at her from the corner of his eye, enjoying her reaction to the screeching of the brakes. The way she shuts her eyes and sits erect in her seat, holding on to the dashboard is her helpless, scared self which irritates him the most.

Lalita answers a call on her cell phone. Mahesh honks. She presses her left hand on her ear, so he honks again and she knows that he has honked to attract her attention and looks at him. Wind up, he signs, so she says bye to Audrey and disconnects the call.

She is already making arrangements for the week, she plans to drag him and Vinodini to Wadi. Vinodini did not seem too pleased about it, and Lalita had told her how it would make Mother happy. She had saved the 'surprise' for this morning, and had told her mother at the airport.

'We will go and stay in the old house, Mamma,' she had beamed and Mother had said, 'Why?'. Just 'why?' There was hope, Mahesh thought, of getting out of this yet, for once the old lady disapproved, that was that.

And here, Lalita was making detailed plans for his daughter to stay with that NGO-type single woman who dares to smoke in front of kids!

'Yeah, I know that Audrey's daughters will be good company for Aphra. But when her grandparents are in the same town — for heaven's sake...' he says, for the second time that day.

Lalita does not say anything. She does up an undone button on Aphra's frock and smoothes down the fabric.

She holds the child close to her chest.

***

Lalita is ten years old. She holds Vinodini, only two year old, on her lap. Vinodini cries that she wants to go for a drive in Baba's car.

But they are in an auto-rickshaw.

The road is rough. The trees cast shadows.

Lalita holds Vinu close to her. Uma Bai, the domestic help, tries to take Vinu on her lap.

Vinu puts her arms around Lalita's neck. Vinu's body is rigid and tense.

She buries her face in Lalita's unruly curls. Lalita smoothens down Vinodini's long, silky, straight hair.

Lalita hums a song. Vinu slowly relaxes. Lalita looks at a tomb. It is surrounded by trees. Clay lamps have been lit all around it.

Vinu's mouth is slightly open. Her body still shakes with occasional sobs, but she is comfortably curled up. Lalita's frock is wet with Vinu's saliva and tears. Vinu is fast asleep.

***

As if suddenly woken up, she looks out of the window and says she thinks she saw her sister on a scooter at the last traffic signal.

He is exasperated. As usual she must have mistaken someone else for Vinodini.

As usual, she has not been listening to him.

Vinodini never listens to anything she says, sometimes, Lalita feels like holding her by the shoulders and telling her how much she loves her, how she is the person she loves the most.

She has always been the person Lalita has loved the most and perhaps that is why she has been kept away from her. Physically, whenever possible, but more importantly in other ways—Vinodini has been very protective about Mother, so has always shown how Lalita is the greatest danger to Mother, how she was a difficult child, an ungrateful adult.

Sad songs are funny, Lalita feels. She finds it ridiculous how the singer lists out the sad things that have been done to him.

To say (or sing!) aloud, to even remember the hurt that has been caused by a loved one is impossible if you truly love the person, she thinks.

To recount details of the suffering inflicted is to list the lapses on the part of the beloved.

How then, can one talk about, remember, details of the suffering, which after all, is nothing but failure of the beloved person?

There have been incidents throughout their childhood.

And now, the relationship has settled down to Vinodini looking down upon her older sister, thinking of her as some sort of an idiot who was a troublesome child and is now a pathetic adult.

A woman without a career. A housewife sticking to a marriage because she has no choice. An overprotective, nagging old-fashioned sister.

'*Am I your bestest sister in the whole world, Akku?*'

Yes, you are, and I have lost you.

***

'You lost your Mother, Lalita.'

Mahesh says. It is he who has received the phone call.

Vinodini and Mahesh have received news of Mother's death. Nobody has bothered to call Lalita.

As if they know that she has already lost Mother quite a while ago.

'She passed away peacefully in her sleep.' Mahesh says.

Yes, she has decided to go to sleep just when Lalita wanted to go to the old house, wanted to talk of the future.

They would have been together as a family. There were reconciliations to be worked out. But first, there would have been arguments, there would have been battles.

Mother has chosen peace.

Mother has chosen to go to sleep, just when Lalita needed her.

Mother has chosen to go to sleep, yet again.

***

To the airport to go to Goa.

From there to Wadi.

But now, not to meet Mother.

Vinodini takes an extra hand-baggage tag and looks at where Lalita is sitting.

Uncomfortably on the edge of a chair, but still looking as if she is the only settled person in that airport crowded with people eating, talking noisily, watching TV, saying goodbyes, looking up at the indicator every time an announcement is made.

Lalita is in no hurry to go, as if she knows she is not going anywhere.

Or, as if she has already taken herself somewhere.

It's best to leave her alone, Mahesh thinks as he steers Vinodini towards the coffee counter. She's probably thinking about her Mother.

***

This woman is not her Mother.

And yet, Lalita does not want the afternoon to end, does not want to go back, does not want to go away from this orchard, from this woman.

This eleven-year-old child who has recently lost her Baba.

This big, warm woman with her saree pallu on her head, going behind the ears, emphasising her coarse features, the wisdom in them.

Jackfruits—green, reachable jackfruits rough on the outside and sweet, nourishing on the inside, like her Khala, she thinks as Khala holds her hand and gently presses it on the thorny surface of the Jackfruit.

'According to Hindu mythology, trees would not fruit unless touched by tree nymphs.'

Khala is Karim Uncle's wife. All the stories from Hindu mythology that Lalita will one day tell her child, she has heard from her Muslim aunt — her Khalajaan.

Khala is like a jackfruit, the child smiles to herself, and Karim Uncle is like this coconut tree, she thinks as her hand caresses the smooth trunk of a coconut palm — tall, strong and elegant.

He is always dressed so impeccably, it is hard to believe that after court work, after a day at his law office, working in this orchard is what he likes to do best.

Khala's orchard still has the tall old coconut trees that Lalita likes. Everywhere else, in Wadi, the shorter, quicker growing palms, the Singapuri Maads are being planted.

Lalita hugs the trunk of a tall tall tree. She is happy that Karim Uncle is her Father's closest friend.

Was.

Thankfully though, Khala still is Lalita's friend.

'Tell me about the tree-women, Khala.'

Khala stops walking. 'Again?' she smiles.

The girl insists, and Khala starts speaking as they walk hand in hand.

'In the holy land, Dryads dwelt under the name of Benat Ya'kob — daughters of Jacob. The trees — even fallen branches of their groves — were never touched, even in a land where wood is scarce."

Scarce wood, scarce food — it is difficult for the child to imagine such a land, looking as she is now, at the bunches of short, fine-skinned bananas.

She holds her face close to the bunch to find her favourite part of the banana plant — the dark purple-red-maroon-brown flower.

'The female flowers do not need to be fertilized to become fruit,' Khala tells her, 'so they stay away from the male and grow farther up the stem.'

So the fleshy, sweet-scented bracts are snugly protecting only the male flower.

The female flower is not protected.

It does not need to be protected because it does not have to be fertilized.

Is there a dryad who blesses it into fruition?

The dryad holds a banana flower close to her face and smells it. She lets go of it and then, touches the female flower. She smiles at this flower—unprotected as she is, for she walks alone.

She walks among the trees.

Lalita walks among the trees. Her bare feet leave a dark red colour in the stream she crosses. She steps back on the red mud and again, lets the stream wash her feet.

She lets the stream wash her hands.

Her hands feel the rough bark, as she hugs a tree.

To hug a big tree, to fall asleep hugging a big tree.

'Told me to talk, and you are dreaming away.' Sometimes, it seems that Khala has an uncanny ability to see sadness even before it touches Lalita. A large rough fist touches Lalita's cheek and opens up suddenly to show a pod of tamarind. Khala pries open the pod with her fingers.

Lalita's tongue runs over her lips.

Her fingers pick a piece of tamarind.

Over her head, there are many tamarinds growing on the tree. Suspended on the almost horizontal branch of a mango tree is a swing. Lalita holds the thick coir rope. She has a fond expression on her face. She obviously remembers something very pleasant. Suddenly, her face is clouded. She lets go of the rope.

Lalita walks fast. She starts running. Finally, she reaches a banyan tree. She looks at the leaves, the accessory roots which go into the soil to form yet another tree. She holds on to one. She is tired.

A whole network of branches, roots, thick foliage. At the centre, an almost circular space.

Lalita enters this space. She kneels down. Her fingers dig into the soil.

Khala's voice fills the breeze that carries secrets from tree to tree.

'A dryad lived in her special tree.

When the tree died so did she.'

The expression on Lalita's face is that of a child wanting her mother.

She sinks down.

She curls up at the root of the tree.

Lalita lies in a foetal position deep within the clump of trees.

***

Lalita is asleep.

Sitting in a chair in the airport lounge. Suddenly, she opens her eyes. She stands up, as if starting to go somewhere. Vinodini walks towards her sister.

Lalita tries to hug her. Vinodini stands awkwardly, clutching her bag and laptop.

She brushes aside the bottle of water offered by Lalita, not once looking at her sister.

Lalita opens the cap of the bottle and this time Vinodini takes it and takes a sip. They look at each other and are about to say something when Mahesh comes. He pats Vinodini's shoulder. He leads her towards the security check entrance. Lalita lifts up two bags and starts walking behind them. They stand in a queue.

Mahesh has to, of course, make an irritating effort to what he thinks is lightening the mood —

'This is a first. Going without first calling up to ask for her permission.'

Vinodini looks at her sister indicating that this is just the kind of remark she expects from him.

'As expected,' he comments, on seeing the small aircraft which she has expected too, though not with the fear of discomfort as he has but with the reassurance that at least the aircraft will be as before.

Pune – Goa flights, the airline has decided, deserve this small plane with the two propeller fans at the wings.

A different aircraft it is, the flight-attendant mentions. Therefore, it is imperative that they listen to the security instructions even though they may all be frequent fliers.

Only Lalita looks at the demonstration with genuine and focussed attention.

This sincere interest comes naturally to mothers of children who have one-minute roles in school concerts.

Caregivers of old people who might say one word indicating a need, or a change of medical condition learned to observe.

Women who talked and nobody looked up to listen to them, wanted to do that.

The carefully uniformed face looks grateful as Lalita listens carefully even when she repeats the same thing over, this time in Hindi.

Familiar fan-things and the wings, like everybody else who is familiar with Lalita do not want to be watched so closely.

'Why do you watch every change of expression?'

What can she do, she has a window seat right on the wings, if she can see every angle, every change, which if carried out to completion, might result in destruction.

Between seeing the slight change and then seeing things come back to safety is the terrible period of knowing what may happen, knowing that she cannot do anything to stop it; yet being in a position where she can see the slightest disturbance, the potential devastation.

To be able to see is to be held responsible.

Responsible for all these people, she smiles to herself, as she sees the other passengers eating. Both sisters have refused the meal, and yet, by habit, the flight attendant has opened the tray meant for Vinodini.

Vinodini pushes back the open tray on the seat in

front. It snaps open. Frustrated, Vinodini bangs it with her fist. A man looks behind through the gap between the seats.

Lalita's hand puts back the tray properly. Lalita reaches out to her sister. Vinodini moves her head away and looks at a newspaper. She is in tears.

Lalita silently mouths, 'Vinu.'

***

'Vinu.'

'You are swinging between two States.'

Her hands hold on to the big stick, just like railway crossing gates. The stick that goes up to let vehicles go from one State to another.

'Now you are in Goa, now you are in Maharashtra,' Akku says.

Lalita pretends to be a smuggler. 'Let's smuggle some liquor in,' Baba says.

Patradevi.

Lalita, her husband and her sister are in Maharashtra now. The three-hour drive from the Goa airport to Wadi is coming to an end and they are at the Patradevi border.

Baba would park the car on the Maharashtra side and walk over to the Goa side.

The duty-free side.

There were many liquor shops just past the gate precisely for this kind of thing. Everybody did it, and the cops turned a blind eye. But while they did it, Baba made a big show of tip-toeing across the border, stealing across the police chowkey, all for Lalita's sake. She loved it.

Partners in crime, friends, Father and daughter, Baba and Lalita.

And then, Baba died.

And now, Mamma is dead.

And so, Patradevi is an ordinary check-post.

But there are still all the extraordinary aspects of this place, they will never change, thinks Lalita as she looks at the red soil that she has missed so much.

***

Kokanchi maati.

The red soil of the Konkan.

Maatitlya goshti.

The stories in the soil.

Red stories?

Blood stories?

The soil was rich in dark stories, which in turn had given rise to all the local sayings, the local superstitions.

A soil rich in stories.

Would the stories come tumbling down now, for they are digging into the earth? Even from the road, mining activity is visible.

Digging equipment. Monstrous avatars of shovels and pickaxes.

Shovels.

Pickaxes.

Curettes.

Curettes used in a dilatation and curettage of the uterus.

Baaichya potaat kaahi tikat naahi.

Nothing is retained in the stomach of a woman.

Who could have thought of this saying ?

About someone whose stomach keeps a person safe till they are ready to face the world?

It is not about babies though, it is about secrets.

A secret can never be safe with a woman.

She has to blurt it out, otherwise it feels as though her stomach will burst.

No secret can stay in a woman's stomach.

Had this saying been made so that women would feel compelled to not keep secrets?

Did the world want to know her secrets?

The secrets that a woman keeps.

The secrets that a woman makes up.

The truth is actually that the world wants to get whatever is inside the woman's stomach.

Mines everywhere.

Penetrating mines.

Nothing is allowed to stay inside a woman.

Baaichya potaat kaahi tikat naahi.

***

Unopposed mines.

Father had tried to oppose the mines.

The mining lobby had been too strong. Father's Party had been bought over. Dr. Patwardhan had been told to keep quiet about the environmental hazards of the mining activity, the displacement of the locals and so on, or lose his ticket. The Party would not make him their candidate for the next Vidhan Sabha elections if he continued his struggle against mining.

He chose his love for the land and so it was decided that he would not represent the constituency in the state legislative assembly.

He chose the well-being of his people and so it was decided that he could not be their leader.

To be so idealistic about a profession that you cannot be allowed to practise it.

To love someone so much that you cannot be allowed to work with them.

To need someone so much that you cannot be allowed to tell them something that needs to be told.

***

'Vinu...' Lalita starts to say something, but they have reached Wadi. She catches her first glimpse of the lake.

'Vinu...'

'Vinu.' Lalita says almost to herself.

Her three-year-old sister has found a new game — covering her Akku's eyes and asking her to guess who it is.

As if anybody else would notice Lalita in her hidden corners in the garden.

As if Vinodini would want to attract the attention of anyone else.

'*Vinu.*' *She says now and holds the child close to herself.* '*Sshh*', *she says and points to the hills. It is raining there. Soon the rain will sweep in towards their house. Between their house and the hills is a lake, and the rain will have to cross that. Lalita loves that brief time when it is not raining in their garden, but the drops are already playing on the lake surface.*

The hills are black-grey now. It is time. She hopes that Vinodini won't start anything now, that she would not want her sister to come away. Lalita likes to see the rain cross the lake to meet her.

But Vinodini holds her finger, pulls her along, as if she wants to take her somewhere, and then lets her go and runs away, telling her sister to catch her.

Choosing to run away and to get lost, and then expecting her Akku to find her.

Her own voice calling out, 'Vinu'.

And the voice of little Vinodini laughing and saying that Lalita will never be able to catch her.

Lalita's memory of the house will forever 'follow' this chase. She will forever run without actually seeing her sister or even her own younger self, through an extremely beautiful, but uncared for house. Run, stop to catch her breath and look up at the old, high wooden ceilings with lovely lamps hanging from them, huge rooms, antique furniture all resounding with the sisters' voices.

Stepping through French windows, running up a winding staircase, she will always find herself in a dark dining room.

She will say 'I can't see you,' really scared now, for Vinodini is nowhere in sight, although her childish laughter can be heard.

She will look around and know that everything else has also drowned in darkness.

***

Light floods the room to show Lalita that Vinodini, Mahesh and Shriram Bhatji are talking at one end of the table.

Shriram Bhatji is a sixty-year-old Hindu priest. He is overtly benevolent in his manner.

Lalita sits at the other end of the table, directly opposite to him. Her face is turned away from them. She has opened the sideboard drawer and is feeling the cutlery. She drops a spoon. Vinodini is irritated at the sound. Vinodini screams at Lalita.

'Clumsy. Stop that and pay attention.'

Lalita grips the spoon tightly and listens.

Shriram Bhatji walks up to Lalita. She is cornered between the sideboard and his body.

'Let her *atma* attain *mukti*, Akku tai.'

Mahesh has his usual concern, 'What will my parents think?'

Shriram Bhatji agrees with him. Their status needs to be taken into account. He says, 'The people, your relatives, will all expect a big funeral.'

Lalita looks overpowered. She manoeuvres her way out of that cell that both men have created with their bodies.

Her head is at the level of Mahesh's attractive chest and Shriram Bhatji's man-boobs, when Bhatji says, 'The people from your village, especially, she after all, brought back the respect, the name...'

Lalita looks up at him, daring him to complete his sentence. Who had destroyed the respect, the name, that Mother saved, she wants to ask.

***

The name.

Indrajeet Mansinghrao Patwardhan.

'Who do they think they are trying to bribe?' Baba is angry.

'They cannot buy...'

'Indrajeet Mansinghrao Patwardhan,' Lalita says and snuggles up to him for he will now tell the story of how her grandfather fought against the British rulers.

A familiar story, one she needn't stay awake to understand.

To fall asleep, to hear it as in a dream.

First really sleep, the cold ghat breeze caressing her cheek.

Then pretend to be asleep when they reach home, so that Baba has to carry her up to her room, put a blanket on her.

Then lie awake wondering what had upset her Baba so much that day.

Why had Baba been called for a meeting to Amboli?

Why did people cut down real forests and then make a garden look like a forest?

A khota-khota forest.

An attenuated simulation.

A forest not fierce, a forest not wonderful.

False red roofs, a modern ceiling inside.

A forest, precious minerals inside.

Men who wanted to dig up those minerals, and for that, cut the forest.

Strangers, who pretended to be Baba's friends, just because his real friends had let him down.

What was so sad about not getting a ticket?

Why did Baba need a ticket to be with his people?

Like the false forest-garden in which it had been held, if only the meeting had been *khota-khota,* everything would have been different.

Khota-khota.

False.

Make-believe.

If she got scared while watching a movie, Baba had told her how it was just *khota-khota;* that it could not harm her.

If only that meeting had not happened.

If only Baba had not allowed hurt to weaken him.

***

Then Baba's death would have been a *khota-khota* thing.

Everything would have been different.

Lesser men like Shriram Bhatji would then have not been allowed to make a derogatory comment about Indrajeet Patwardhan.

She looks at Vinodini, who also seems to have been affected by what Bhatji has left unsaid, but affected in a different way — she is not angry, she is ashamed, and this further angers Lalita.

But one look at her sister, and as usual she decides to spare her of even discomfort.

'Whatever Vinodini wants,' she says.

Vinodini shakes her forefinger at Lalita, like Mother used to.

'I know what this bitch wants. She wants Mamma to be thrown into an incinerator.'

Lalita lifts her hand to touch her, 'So much hatred?'

Vinodini turns her face away.

Lalita tries to hold her hand.

Vinodini pulls it away and looks at her wrist.

A scar.

Vinodini touches the scar with her finger.

'You'd stop whining about hatred, if only you knew what your so-called LOVE does to people.'

Lalita gives up, sighs and leaves the room.

***

Lalita enters the inner living room. Vinodini runs past her to Mother's dead body.

Vinodini goes and hugs Mother's body.

Lalita looks at her garlanded photograph kept nearby. Mother is a powerful, handsome woman.

Lalita and Anuradha Auntie look at each other. They remember an attractive woman, so particular about her dress, her looks.

They remember the election campaign, the changed dressing style, how the chiffons had given way to printed pure silk sarees. Never handloom ones, though they would have been more apt for the new role —

'Those starched sarees will make me look fat, Anuradha.'

And that big vermillion mark on her forehead.

'A bigger *tikli*, Anuradha, I want it to be seen from a distance.'

Standing in a jeep, huge sunglasses hiding her expression, but the body poised and looking forward to being the centre of attraction.

'Am I looking okay? The whole town will see me.'

The whole town will see her today.

Anuradha Auntie reaches out to put *kumkum* on Mother's forehead but is stopped by Attya.

'This *abhagi*, did she have the fortune to die with a bright forehead?"

Attya looks at Mother's face, she is sorry for her, but in a condescending way.

Lalita keeps Mother's glasses by her body.

'Fortunate for us though to have at least one parent to see us to adulthood,' she says concentrating on the watch she is strapping on to Mother's wrist.

Attya pulls out her own *mangalsutra* from somewhere inside her blouse and displays it on her chest even as she looks at Lalita who can see how she appears to her Aunt — no *kumkum* on her forehead, no *mangalsutra*, etc.

Attya starts her usual refrain about how the symbols of *Soubhagya*, good fortune, the good fortune of being married and having a husband who is alive at that.

Just as Lalita can see how she appears to Attya, the other women in the room begin to see it too.

Lalita is visibly uncomfortable.

That is enough provocation for Attya to muster the guts to continue her ranting about how she has heard that Lalita does not want Mother to have a proper religious funeral.

Ignoring that, as if she has not heard, as if she has been putting this argument together, Lalita, in a pleasant tone, says how it is good that Attya brought this up for if Lalita, a *Soubhagyavati*, can choose not to wear the vermillion mark, Mother, a widow can have it on her forehead, because she had liked it, because she had not been allowed to wear it after she became a widow and surely, a dead body was beyond all rules, was it not?

Now it is Attya's turn to ignore, and bring back the discussion to why Lalita does not wear a *mangalsutra*.

'Pseudo-bloody-secular pretensions,' says Vinodini as if in reply to Attya's question.

Lalita looks surprised that Vinodini is with Attya on this whole issue about *mangalsutras*, that she feels that it is some kind of pretentiousness that her sister has never liked that piece of jewellery.

Vinodini walks to the refrigerator and opens it. She has followed her sister into the kitchen not to reprimand her for answering back to Attya as it looks to the others, but because she cannot bear being alone in the same room as her relatives.

Alone, means being without *her* Akku, so going back to her childhood habit, she has simply trailed behind Lalita.

***

Vinodini, two years old, tightens her arms around Lalita's neck.

Lalita is kneeling behind their mother, on the bed.

Madhav Kaka wipes off the kumkum from Mother's forehead.

Lalita holds her mother by the shoulders.

She wants to hit her uncle as his hand approaches her mother's breasts, his fingers spread and bent to grasp.

She looks questioningly at Mother. Mother's eyes are closed.

Madhav Kaka's fingers curl around the necklace which has always been around Mother's neck, as if a part of her. No matter what earrings, bangles she chose to wear, she has never taken it off.

Madhav Kaka breaks her Mother's mangalsutra.

Mother cries out in pain.

***

Lalita touches the back of her neck and readjusts her saree *padar*.

She looks at her sister.

The collar seems to bother Vinodini, she touches the back of her neck in exactly the same way.

Lalita smiles.

Vinodini looks for something in the refrigerator. Lalita opens a *dabba* and serves some upma in a plate. She keeps it on the kitchen table.

She taps Vinodini's shoulder and closes the refrigerator. Vinodini goes and sits at the table.

Spoon in hand, she waits for Lalita to leave before she can eat.

And Lalita leaves, she wants Vinodini to eat.

***

Lalita looks at Mother's body being prepared for the funeral. On the adjacent terrace, preparations are going on for the 'bath'. Big copper vessels are filled with water. A set of clothes is kept on a wooden platform.

A priest walks by Lalita as she goes across the room to the terrace. She blocks the doorway with her hand and indicates that he should not enter. The priest looks at her face. He then looks beyond her. Vinodini stands in the doorway. The priest goes back outside.

Vinodini follows her sister to the terrace.

Lalita's back is turned towards Vinodini. She leans against the railing. Downstairs, in the courtyard, a big crowd waits.

A bamboo stretcher is ready. Flowers and garlands in baskets.

The crisp, white new cloth neatly folded.

In contrast lies the rope.

Lalita leans over a little.

The coils of rope look scary.

Lalita starts leading everyone out. They are startled. They start leaving by the staircase leading downstairs.

Vinodini turns away. She looks down. Vinodini becomes conscious of the fact that some people are looking at them.

How the two sisters must look to them.

Lalita distressed, almost hysterical.

Vinodini dignified, controlled.

She speaks softly now. But she holds Lalita's wrist firmly.

'Anything physical, anything personal for her, you always wanted to do it alone.'

Lalita's arms hang loosely. She looks too weak to say anything.

What else was I allowed, she wants to ask, but does not have to for Vinodini is already pointing to Lalita, her open palm moving up and down.

'What else are you capable of?   Look at you. Shuffling...'

...through the present, weighed down by the past?

'The past.' Vinodini goes on, 'So you don't have to actually do anything in the present. Always the past under a microscope.'

What can she do?

The ability to see, understand and experience is all she has. Some lives are like that. One terrible thing happens, they face it, and then, that in itself becomes their job. The people downstairs can see them, she realises, and tries to free her hand.

Vinodini lets go of her wrist. She realises too that people can see them, that her sister is concerned that people don't see them like that.

Full sleeved frocks to hide scratch marks which may have been made by the dog, bruises which she may have got when she fell off the step-ladder. For a fleeting moment, there is some sympathy in her eyes.

Lalita sees that and reaches out the hand she has pulled away just a moment ago.

Greedy for affection, sensitive to even the possibility of affection, reaching out, begging, she is pathetic, thinks Vinodini and moves away from Lalita.

'Vinu.'

Vinodini is her defiant self again. She walks towards the living room.

***

Lalita stands in the doorway and looks into the room. Vinodini is leading everybody out. Lalita goes and sits down near the body.

Vinodini talks to Nakusa. Nakusa is fifty-two-year-old, with thick, matted hair that has never been combed out.

Yellow powder smeared horizontally across her forehead, her clothes are dusty. There is something strange about her.

Vinodini seems to fear her, she looks away even while she talks to Nakusa.

'...but the rituals will be carried out. And a proper *sutak* observed for thirteen days.'

Nakusa's gaze accompanies the *agarbatti* smoke that wafts towards the doorway and washes across Lalita's face.

'For her, the *sutak* has been going on for twenty-four years,' Nakusa says.

***

Nakusa lives in *Bahercha Wada.*

The child has never cycled off alone this far from home before.

Lalita cycles through a small town.

She reaches the outskirts.

The town makes no efforts to disguise the way it segregates people.

There is no attempt at political correctness.

This part of town is called Bahercha Wada – the outer neighbourhood. Every town has people who, if they want to live, have to stay out of the way of the powerful. People of a lower caste, lesser religion. People who do 'dirty' jobs. This 'dirt' comes from the higher, greater, cleaner who live in the main town. However, the main town does not want these people to live with them.

These people who are supposed to stay out, live in the outer neighbourhood the Bahercha Wada.

The dwellings look poorer as compared to the rest of the town. Children look at her bicycle with envy as she asks them for some directions.

She needs directions to this place she has been to before, as she has never gone there alone.

With Zaid, she feels that she knows the way, but finding it alone is always a problem.

A girl points to the top of a hill.

Lalita cycles away through the outer part of this outer part of the town, and then, the forest.

Lalita alights at the foot of the hill. She walks uphill. The light begins to fade. The slightest sound of an animal or even the breeze in the trees frightens her. She walks on.

At the top of the hill, she feels, not for the first time, that she should have come with him but Zaid would have laughed at her.

Although he joins his friend in some of her make-believe games, to him, they are just that – games.

What would he do if he knew that they meant much more to her, that in these games, Lalita looked for something to believe in.

In a clearing is a small temple.

Some stones are arranged to resemble a human form.

The face of a terrifying female deity.

Nakusa is in a trance. Her matted hair left loose, eyes closed, she is engrossed in a slow, wild dance.

Lalita looks at her. She leans her cycle against a tree.

The sound of a hen being slaughtered scares her.

A breeze makes her hair wild, she has washed it and has run away here before anybody has a chance to tame it.

Lalita sits down at a distance. She clutches the money in her hand. A family sits in front of Nakusa. The man offers some money to her. She puts out her hand, but the money is snatched by an older woman.

Nakusa talks to the family. Her eyes are closed. 'A spirit talks through her.' She opens her eyes and sees Lalita. She gestures that the family should leave. She goes to Lalita and helps her up. She starts leading her away from the temple. The old woman looks on disapprovingly.

Lalita is a little afraid of Nakusa's mother.

'I got the money,' she whispers proudly.

Nakusa laughs and keeps walking. They walk downhill. Nakusa points to a Bharadwaj bird.

At the foothill, Nakusa climbs onto the bicycle and indicates that the child should sit on the carrier. Lalita smiles, and hops on. They ride away in total darkness. Lalita puts her hand around Nakusa's waist.

The matted hair, which from a distance looks like something to be feared, is rough but comforting, and the child lays her cheek on it.

Kharkareet, rough.

She remembers how once when she had said the word, Baba had repeated it, emphasising the sounds, telling her how the word sounded, even felt like what it meant.

Now, speeding over the bumpy road, she closes her eyes and repeats the sounds in tune with the jolts.

Kharrr-kha-rrreet.

Rough but comforting, like Father's morning face.

'Baba'.

Nakusa sits up straighter, pushes her back closer to the child.

'Your Baba's spirit is in your heart and you can always talk to him.'

They pass the family that Lalita had seen at the temple. The couple walks at the very edge of the road like people used to staying out of the way. They walk wearily, close together.

Nakusa returns the man's greeting, and turns her face back slightly to talk to Lalita.

'I know, they too will not need a medium, very soon.'

Night.

They stop outside a house.

As Nakusa is handing the bicycle to Lalita, a little girl runs out, holds the edge of her mother's saree and stands shyly behind her.

Nakusa pulls her and says she should greet Akka. Lalita Akka is the girl from the big house, so grimy thin hands are folded in a shy awestruck Namaste.

Lalita, who is only a few years older to this child does not know how to react to the Namaste, and puts out a small-town-convent-school hand, which is not shaken.

Nakusa wraps both the girls in a warm, sweaty hug.

'If Jana gets books and Lalita a bit of magic...'

She turns her closed fist in the air and opens it suddenly in front of Lalita's face.

A string of plastic beads has 'appeared' there. She ties it around Lalita's neck.

***

Lalita puts on a string of pearls around Mother's neck. She wonders what Jana does now. She wishes she could ask Nakusa.

Lalita looks at Nakusa, at her dark, callused hand, as it applies pressed powder on Mother's face.

She has not spoken to the woman for ten years, and yet, on hearing of Nalini's death, Nakusa has come to help the family.

As she had when Aphra was born.

It was the fourth day, and Mahesh had finally found the time to come to see his child. *He had driven through the night.* Had he driven through the night, because the only thing Lalita had kept repeating in their telephone conversations was 'Please do not drive in the ghat at night'? Had it begun already, then? Were not the initial years at least free of all that? Lalita likes to remember that her daughter was born in a time of love.

Anyway, he had reached at nine in the morning when Nakusa had been giving the baby an oil massage. After the initial look of disapproval, he had not paid much attention.

He had missed her, her body and he had ignored the baby to hug his wife, to whisper into her ear.

Whispers about what he wanted to do to her, what he was going to do to her when they got home.

Maybe it was unfair that she was irritated at this kind of talk. Had she insulted his affection? But then, she wanted him to talk about what *she* had done. What Lalita had done was that she had given birth to his baby.

Yes, it had been affection but his touches had become more intimate when the baby was taken for its bath. Lalita wished he would just hold her as she caught a short nap, now that the baby was taken off her hands for a while.

The baby had to be fed often in the night and Lalita felt drained, sore.

She had wanted to tell her husband all this, when suddenly, he had squeezed her breast.

And Lalita had slapped him on his face.

She will remember this forever.

Was this, then, the first time that she had discovered that she could be repulsed by her husband's touch?

Perhaps, but she also remembers this for another reason.

She had been reminded of this every time he had hit her in the years afterwards.

She had started the physical violence. The humiliation, the hurt. To feel enough hatred to want to inflict physical hurt in an intimate relationship.

She had made hitting a reality in their marriage.

She remembered this every time she was hurt after their fights.

She remembered her slap long after she had forgotten the pain in the milk — laden breast which he had squeezed it that day.

And she had known that Mahesh too would remember. She had known, seeing his anger that day, the anger that he had vented on Nakusa.

She had put the baby in its cradle and gone back to get the *dhoop*.

Lalita liked the pleasant smelling smoke that emanated from a little clay bowl that Nakusa carried. Her hands waved the smoke into hidden corners, which somehow seemed clean after she did this.

'How can you allow such a barbaric practice? What will it do to my child's lungs?' Mahesh had shouted at Lalita.

'Who is this woman? How can you let her bathe the baby? Can't you see how unhygienic she is?'

It was her matted hair, a sign of what she was, what she did.

Black under her nails, from the coal she must have collected for the *dhoop*.

Her cracked feet.

Her face.

Her eyes waiting for Lalita to say something.

But Lalita had gestured with her hand that she should go away.

And take with her the care, the service, the love that she had brought to Lalita and her baby.

Perhaps it was because of what had just happened between her and Mahesh. Another thing would have been too much to handle. She would talk to Nakusa later.

But the maid who was sent to *Bahercha Wada* came back saying that Nakusa wouldn't bathe the baby any more.

Had her pride in traditional knowledge been insulted? Lalita had thought, for Nakusa had not come back to the house after that and known that it was much more than that.

Her one gesture had sent away the woman who had been a fierce friend.

Had Lalita lost this 'fierce', strong part of herself when Nakusa went away that day?

She had lost another caring woman in exactly the same way. Even then, her family's attitude towards Other people, Lower people, Other religions, Other castes had been the same.

Family members who would themselves never care, seemed to have an opinion about the people who did care.

Prejudices about religion, about caste had made a Brahmin girl Untouchable.

Not-touchable by two women who loved her.

To be touched only by legitimately allowed people and then to be touched by them even if she did not love them.

Legitimate family could choose the persons who could be allowed to love someone they were supposed to love.

It was love that had won over pride, and ten years since she was rejected, Nakusa had come back.

Unaware of how extraordinary a woman she was, how much her strong presence meant to Lalita, the women in the family were glad she was here to do the things deemed ordinary.

To dress a body that had been Mother, to wash a dead body – ordinary things are they?

Nakusa gathers Nalini's saree from the floor. A new saree has been draped around Mother. Lalita pins up the *padar* to the blouse.

Mother's ankle is exposed. Lalita covers it up with the saree. Her hand stays on mother's leg.

***

Lalita is ten years old. She sits on the bed and keeps her hand on Mother's leg.

Mother turns on her side and looks away.

'He doesn't even like those.' The child now appeals to Khala.

Anuradha Auntie holds a set of some formal, probably never worn clothes, which belonged to father.

Attya looks heavenwards, 'Doesn't'? Has Attya already begun to think of her brother in the past tense?

Lalita pulls at Mother's shoulder.

'We know what clothes he likes, don't we Mamma?'

Khala tries to make Nalini take notice of her daughter.

As soon as she starts to say something, Attya tells her not to interfere, she does not know their customs, she is a Muslim after all.

Madhav Kaka agrees and puts on his grating polite tone 'These are religious ceremonies.'

Religious ceremonies were poojas, festivals, how can this be a religious ceremony? Baba is dead.

Madhav Kaka tells Khala 'You might touch something.'

Lalita feels Khala's hands let go of her shoulder.

A Brahmin girl made Untouchable.

Not-touchable by a woman who loved her.

To be touched only by legitimately allowed people and then to be touched by them even if she did not love them.

Mother gestures to Anuradha Auntie that Lalita should be taken away. Anuradha Auntie taps Lalita on the shoulder and calls her out. Mother is fed up of Lalita. She shakes her head.

'Stop talking like a mad person,' says Anuradha Aunty and leads Lalita out of the room.

Lalita keeps a distance between Anuradha Auntie and herself as soon as she realises that they are going towards Shriram Bhatji and Madhav Kaka.

Anuradha Auntie hands the clothes to Shriram Bhatji who says, 'Madhavbhau, body is not in any condition to be brought here and bathed by us.'

Madhav Kaka has not planned to do it himself.

'After the post mortem, the boys there can do all that.'

Shriram Bhatji holds out the clothes.

'Send these outside with someone. He's coming at seven'o clock — that mahar.'

Mahar — a harijan caste. The priest has an irritating habit of referring to everyone by their caste.

Lalita takes the clothes from his hand.

'His name is Vasant Kaka,' she says.

***

Lalita waits near the garage at the back of the house, with these clothes in a bag. Dark clouds have gathered in the sky.

Vasant, a ward attendant gets off his bicycle.

She hands over the bag and indicates that those clothes are for him.

He hangs it on the handle bar and from the other side, gets a plastic bag.

He shows her the neatly ironed green surgical scrub clothes. He will dress Sir in these, he assures her. Lalita touches her Father's initials embroidered on the top left of the shirt. She puts a pen in the shirt's pocket.

Lalita hands him a stethoscope. She can barely speak. He nods. She holds out a yellow envelope. The poor man is in tears. He takes the letter.

'Akka, whenever you call up, I always pass your message properly. No?' he asks, and without waiting for a reply, cycles away.

***

Lalita walks into a small garden at the side of the house.

Advocate Kanvinde has apparently been speaking to Mahesh and Vinodini for some time.

'You will get a good price because of the Konkan railway and all...'

The railway has finally reached Wadi. Dr. Patwardhan had spoken about the need for it in the state assembly.

He did not live to see the little stations, the two tracks that ran in the green land, the tunnels.

The Konkan railway had been so dear to him. That would link Wadi to the big city. But Wadi should not try and be like a big city, he had insisted, the land should be saved. He reprimanded other local politicians who turned brokers for rich fertile land. He took a stand against the beginning of mining in the district.

'Whatever anyone might say.'

'We know, don't we?'

***

Lalita seems to be looking for someone.

She goes to the fence for the purpose that has brought her here in the first place. She has definitely not come to the back garden to listen to Kanvinde.

Lalita looks at the large quantities of dried leaves in the garden.

Dried, not dead.

Dried leaves make a bonfire.

A bonfire gives warmth.

And stories.

The brown leaves have formed a blanket throughout the grounds.

The stories are covered.

The rustle of leaves, stories trying to make themselves heard.

The sound of footsteps, Lalita still waits.

'There she is dreaming away. I don't blame your mother for not even considering her,' says Mahesh to Vinodini.

'What does she need money for? Wife of the leading cardiologist in town!' his sister-in-law agrees.

Lalita is suddenly alert.

She looks shocked, she hears about the will for the first time. It is obvious that mother has left everything to Vinodini.

Lalita feels hurt, but somehow, although she has never thought about the house as 'property', never thought of money, it is as if she has always expected this to happen.

'*You are my waaras, Lalita, you will inherit all this.*'

It was not some property that he had spoken about. They were standing together on a stage. He had just finished his speech, it was the last day for canvassing.

They had stood together. How could they leave, when the clapping refused to stop?

His warm face showed what he felt for them.

Pretending is no good; they see through that.

You have to really love your people.'

The clapping filled her head.

Lalita had felt elated, proud.

And, although Baba had always said that feelings of power were wrong, his ancestors had been royal family, he was one of them, hoping they would allow him to speak about their problems, the little girl had felt like a princess that day.

The little girl had felt like a princess that day.

Today, the woman seems small and vulnerable.

Baba's people, her people.

They have gathered on the grounds beyond the garden. They talk quietly amongst themselves. Earthen pots of water have been kept under the mango trees. The older men help themselves to water and sit in the shade under the trees.

Baba did not live to be an old man.

Baba's people, her people.

***

He had done a lot for his people but what Baba had really wanted to do had been left behind. He could not give time to his surgery, to research.

'You become a *real* Doctor, beta.' He had said to Zaid.

'Give Lalita to me when she grows up, Nalini.' Khala had said one day-only half-jokingly.

Mother had looked insulted. She had made it obvious, clear that she thought the idea preposterous. Perhaps to lighten the atmosphere a little, but also to show how her son was in every way equal to the Patwardhans, Khala had said to Father.

'*Apne Indrajeet Kaka ke jaise doctor banna chhahta hai...*' (He wants to be a doctor like his Indrajeet Uncle).

Baba had looked at Zaid.

'You become a real doctor *beta.*'

***

The real doctor.

It's really the doctor.

For a moment she thinks she has imagined him standing there.

Among the mourners dressed in white is an outsider — the doctor in jeans and a black shirt. It is Zaid.

Zaid and Lalita stand on either side of the hedge.

She puts out her hand. He places a small piece of driftwood in her palm. For the first time, Lalita cries.

They stand there for a while. It starts drizzling. They walk towards the house.

'If you Have to play with that boy, at least see that you stay out in the verandah. Please don't get him inside the house.'

So they stop in the verandah, even today, when she knows he has driven twenty hours to get here, that she should ask him inside, he would want to freshen up. But staying in the verandah is important.

What if his visits are stopped altogether if they disobey ?

So they stop, put their elbows on the wooden grill, and look out.

Lalita leans over the grill to stretch out a hand to feel the drops of water on her palm. Zaid comes and stands a little behind her.

Before starting to draw the mehendi pattern, it is important to get your palms clean.

Lalita looks at the rain.

Zaid looks at her.

They sit on cane chairs. Zaid pours a cup of tea. He looks at Vinodini talking to Kanvinde.

He gives Lalita the cup. He is concerned about her. It is so difficult to decipher her. Lalita laughs. Zaid wonders why. Lalita is amused. Lalita's hands caress the leaves of a *mehendi* bush. She smells her hand.

***

Before starting to draw the mehendi pattern, it is important to get your palms clean.

Lalita, all of sixteen now, still obeys the rule.

She has scrubbed her hands clean and holds them out before her, taking care not to touch anything before Khala inspects them.

Lalita sits on a windowsill in the huge kitchen of a big house. She looks out of the window, lost in thoughts. In the garden, Khala picks lemons from a tree. Khala is a big, strong woman with kind eyes. She gestures that Lalita should come out into the sun.

In the garden, Khala hands her the bowl full of lemons and makes her smell them.

She plucks a red hibiscus flower. Khala removes a hairpin from her own hair and uses it to put the flower in Lalita's unruly curls.

Lalita hugs Khala. She covers her face with Khala's saree pallu even as she is dragged along to a corner of the courtyard where Khala still has the old-fashioned slab of stone that she grinds her special masalas on.

Now, she moves the stone aside and puts green leaves on the slab, the paata. After years of use, the paata has sunk into a little concavity in the centre.

Colour juice.

Lalita waits for this first moment in the grinding process when the leaves indicate what they are about.

The promise of colour.

Khala's strong hands crush the mehendi leaves on the paata. Lalita adds fresh leaves.

Khala's daughters rush in asking for something. They throw themselves on Khala's shoulders and say 'Ammi'. Lalita silently mouths the word 'Ammi'. This does not escape Khala's notice.

'Nobody is to bother me when I get this rare time with my favourite daughter.'

The two children run away.

'What they want is all they can think of,' she tells Lalita.

Lalita leans behind and laughs. Khala playfully hits the child with the back of her hand.

'It's better than being like you. You only think of what your Vinu wants.'

'I want the books you have brought from Belgaum,' Lalita

remembers that permission to spend the day at Khala's house has been gained for a specific purpose.

'That other bookworm must be waiting for you in the library.'

Lalita gets up to leave. Khala raises a handful of the ground mehendi to Lalita's nose. The girl inhales deeply.

Khala starts applying mehendi on Lalita's palms. Lalita sits cross-legged in front of Khala. She looks at the door as if she has heard someone. She gets up and runs.

Running in corridors symbolises freedom.

It is a path with doors on both sides, but there is no obligation to enter any of the rooms.

The doors are there always, but the path is free, there is no duty to stop, no compulsion to even look into any door.

***

Lalita stops running only at the library door. Zaid is a tall, intelligent, twenty-year-old, with thick glasses. He puts down the book he's been reading and stands up.

Lalita holds out her hands in front of him.

He looks at the pattern.

He inhales deeply.

The smell of mehendi.

They look at each other.

There is a deep feeling here.

Neither will say how much they have missed the other.

Each one will decide to stop looking at the other as soon as they realise they have been staring, for the other will know it too.

Lalita is the first to look away.

Suddenly, she puts on a casual manner.

'I didn't know you were here,' she says exactly in the same put-on don't-care way that she had last year.

She has not changed, she has been here all the time.

He, however, has changed in the past year. He has been away, and come back taller and seems grown-up to her.

The retort to her 'I didn't know you were here' used to be something different, she has forgotten what it was. Now,

'I didn't know you were here.'

'But I knew you'd come here.'

Lalita looks at the bookcase, blushing. This too, is new.

'I was looking for…'

She mechanically reads the title of the first book she spots on the shelf- Under the Greenwood Tree by Thomas Hardy.

Zaid always 'catches' her at all her pretences.

'When did you break the "only women authors" rule?'

'Since you stopped getting me driftwood.'

Zaid gets a beautifully shaped piece of driftwood out of his pocket. She presses her forearm on a pointed branch.

He looks at her and is about to say something. Khala comes with a parcel wrapped in brown paper. Zaid's manner becomes brisk again.

'Ammi, she's come into the library with that messy stuff on her hands. If even a drop gets on my books...'

He goes out of the room. Khala holds out the book parcel. Lalita's hands have mehendi on them.

With the back of her finger, Lalita touches Khala's glass bangles.

'They say that Zaid is his father's son, but you didn't give birth to him...'

Khala pulls a disobedient curl lower on the child's face, 'How does it matter?' she says.

For the first time, this has been brought up and Khala is not upset. Nor does she stay too long with the thought that somebody has been gossiping about her marriage in front of this child.

She is happy that Lalita wants to know about her Zaid.

That first moment of happiness at the possibility of love between these two children carries with it the fear that Khala will live with as that friendship, that love, progresses.

But now, happily, she raises her eyebrows in her usual 'So what do you think, Lalita?' gesture.

And, the child in her 'I agree with you totally' way that is part of this little ritual they have, repeats what her Khala has said, 'How does it matter?'

Lalita touches her forehead to Khala's.

***

How does it matter?

Lalita touches the frown line between Zaid's eyebrows.

'When you even feel like her.'

Zaid holds her hand.

For a moment, he can see an intricate pattern in wet mehendi.

That day, when he had come home after his second year MBBS exams, she had allowed his mother to finally make that intricate henna pattern, she had held on to those silly dots till then.

There was childishness even in her attempts to seem grown-up, her attempt to feign surprise after she ran into the library looking for him.

'I didn't know you were here.'

'But I knew you'd come here.'

He had wanted to hold her.

He had wanted to tell her that he had gone to bed with a classmate called Shabnam, had tried to go to bed with her that is.

And had failed.

And then cried like a baby calling Lalita's name.

Shabnam had been kind, loving even, but he had worried that she would tell her friends about his 'failure', that the girls would laugh at him.

He had felt shame and had waited for the exams to get over so that he could go and tell Lalita about it.

She had ran into the library, like a child and not only had he known that it would not be possible to share this with her, but had felt guilty at wanting to burden her with his shame.

He had been disappointed at the stint with Shabnam, but his real 'failure' was with Lalita — knowing that he could not touch the girl he had called out to that night when he had tried to be with another, when he had tried to make love for the first time.

He tried to take Lalita away.

Take her out of the games she was busy playing with his sisters. Zaid and Lalita had always brushed the two girls off and wandered off on their own.

Today, she told those pesky kids to stay.

She used them to hide from him.

The four year age difference between him and his friend had never come in the way.

Now suddenly, that he was twenty and wanted to talk seriously for the first time, she became the sixteen-year-old who did not want to listen.

Her put-on childishness was an affront.

Or, was it a defence?

***

Childishness, innocence, ignorance as defence.

An adult woman pretending to have no part in adult discussions.

What is she guarding herself against now, Zaid wonders, irritated at her.

'Why are you not with Vinodini and Mahesh?'

She is surprised that he talks to her so sternly. She realises that he has seen through her disinterested act.

She knows that he can guess that she is being wronged in some way and that she is not strong enough to set it right, that instead of trying to, she retreats into this shell.

She is touched that he cares enough to observe all this, and would like to stand up for herself, even if it is just to respect his concern for her.

But to be childish is comfortable, Lalita thinks as she looks at the lawyer who is reading something out to Vinodini and Mahesh.

'Kanvinde does not like me. As if realising our relative importance, he talks to me once for every ten times that he talks to Mahesh and Vinodini.'

Zaid looks at Kanvinde loosening his tie. In this heat, the lawyer sweats in his black suit.

'Do you really want Kanvinde to like you?'

Lalita stands up. Zaid looks in the direction that she is staring at. Vinodini walks towards them.

'No Zaid, I want Ma to love me.'

Vinodini looks resentfully at her sister as she gives her some papers and then smiles at Dr. Zaid.

'The secret society is still going strong, I see.'

He smiles back at her and they converse politely.

The 'not-for-babies' plans that they kept little Vinu from are not the secrets Lalita is thinking about.

Always for me — the secrets; she wonders what Mother is entrusting her with this time.

***

Mother gives a bunch of keys to her ten-year-old daughter.

She indicates that nobody should lay their hands on them.

Mother in a white saree is lying on a bed.

She has all signs of being recently widowed and in mourning.

Mother closes her eyes as an aunt enters the room. The aunt looks at mother and goes out again.

'The poor wife has been sedated. You will have to talk to the daughter.'

Mother opens her eyes. Lalita keeps the keys in her pocket. Nobody should be allowed to open their cupboards, nobody should find the key.

'The poor wife has been sedated. You will have to talk to the daughter.'

If Mother is the poor wife, is there a rich wife?

Or, is the daughter rich?

Rich daughter, big girl now, trusted with important things.

Big girl, not afraid of anything.

Or anybody.

Not even policemen.

Is the daughter a bad girl that the policemen have come to arrest her?

No.

Policemen protect.

She knows that, she is a big girl, she is Akku.

Silly little Vinu was scared of Baba's bodyguards and hadn't Baba said that they were here to protect?

They are here to protect her from the terrible things that seem to be happening today.

***

The protector looks like a hunter.

Hunters wear safari-suits.

Hunters like Shikaari Shambhu.

Tinkle comics have to be neatly bound in volumes for when Vinu will learn to read.

Then Vinu will also know that hunters are bad people.

Shikaari Shambhu is not to be feared, the animals always escape.

The hunter in Tinkle misses his target.

He does not seem to know what hunters have to do.

He misses the point.

This one comes straight to it.

'Did their fight disturb you last night?'

'No. I was asleep.'

'Were you always asleep when they fought?'

There is no need to feel uncomfortable, policemen help children.

If you are lost in a crowded place always find a policeman.

'Yes.'

'Okay, so, they used to fight often.'

The keychain is made of sandalwood.

Sandal soaps, a small bottle of sandalwood oil, Mother.

If she can get the keychain out of her pocket and smell it, it will be like burying her face in Mother's lap.

But Mother did not want Lalita's head on her lap.

The keys cannot be brought out of the pocket, they have to be protected.

Lalita is the protector.

'So, they used to fight often?'

'I did not say that.'

Not heeding her, the safari suit continues. 'Was there some new name mentioned in the fight?'

Then he turns to the other policeman.

'Why NEW? This must have been going on for quite some time now.'

The other policeman is a younger man in uniform. He has been sitting quietly, taking notes. He takes this question as permission to take part in the proceedings.

He gets up and gives Lalita his chair. People give Baba their chair. She must be doing alright. She is a big girl.

Are big girls supposed to know what has been going on?

And what do new names mean?

New people?

Or old people with new names?

The young, uniformed policeman has his name written on his chest.

T-A-M... no, it must be Tom, but there is a b-

'Our Lalita is a bit of a tomboy, I am afraid,' Mother often says to relatives.

Boys are boys. Bad girls are tomboys.

How can this policeman be called that?

'Why is there no relative with her?' he asks.

The hunter does not pay attention to him. He puts one hand on the back of the chair.

Standing was better.

So this is how safari suits smell — sweat mixed with

*the maidservant's powder and the whiff that enters the car
window when they pass the men's bathroom.*

*'For how long have you known that your father was having
an affair?'*

'What is an affair?' asks Lalita.

*She stands up. The police officer looks her up and down.
Lalita moves towards the bedroom door.*

The hunter grins lewdly and turns to his colleague.

'Tambe, why don't you tell her the meaning?'

'Why is there no relative with her?' says Tom, Tambe again.

Safari-suit holds out small pieces of burnt cloth.

'Your father's body was totally naked.'

He looks at her face for a reaction.

Lalita is on the verge of tears.

*'These are some pieces of cloth we found there. Do you
recognise them?'*

*Lalita holds the cloth pieces in her hand — blue cotton
cloth with a pattern of checks.*

She starts crying.

*She is crying because the only cloth that the hunter could
find 'there' is bits of the collar — the blue checks with canvas
inside has remained because of the thick canvas.*

The rest of Baba's blue shirt, where is it?

The blue shirt with checks.

The picnic shirt.

The Sunday shirt.

Baba has gone for a picnic without her?

'Let's move to the post mortem place. I want to wind up by six,' says Tambe and walks towards Lalita to take the cloth pieces from her.

The child slips a piece into her pocket. He takes the rest, puts them in a small plastic bag, and steers safari out of the room.

Lalita softly calls out Mamma's name. The door of Mother's room is closed. She touches the cloth inside her pocket.

The relatives that the policemen had kept asking for, the relatives that were not found suddenly appear now.

Lalita is taken to the bathroom.

Three aunties and one servant to bathe one little girl.

Is she so dirty? And she can bathe herself, so why are they here? Will they expect her to take off her frock?

They don't.

Attya pushes her shoulders down and she's sitting on the square stone on which Umabai bangs bangs bangs the clothes clean.

Attya pours water on her from afar like she would bathe a dog, Lalita knows how Attya does not like dogs; or maybe she just does not want to get wet.

The blue checks will get wet.

Lalita holds her hand in her pocket and shivers. Anuradha Auntie pours a bucketful of water on her head.

Lots of water will make the shirt very wet.

Had lots of fire burnt it too?

Fire poured on Baba?

Baba on fire?

The child sits with her knees drawn close to her body.

***

Lalita, thirty-four years old, sits with her knees drawn close to her body.

Vinodini protests at the temperature of the water, the idea that people can watch as she washes, that people can actually put mugs of water on her.

Lalita is entirely passive. She has gone through this before, as a bucket of water is poured on her.

The two sisters go through the ritual bath under the watchful eyes of some aunts.

Lalita looks around.

She can hear a baby crying.

***

Mother has placed baby Vinu on her outstretched legs. She pours steaming hot water on her.

Eight-year-old Lalita gets up. She had been sitting on an upturned copper vessel.

She whispers something in Mother's ear.

Mother smiles.

'It is not broken, it is an inverted nipple.'

Lalita giggles.

She puts her finger in the baby's palm.

The baby curls its fingers around it.

'How do both of us have it on the left side?'

'Because both of you are a part of your Mamma.'

'But what does it mean Mamma?'

The domestic help brings in the dhoop. Mother holds the baby over it.

Mother's face is red and tired.

'It means that nurturing our daughters is going to be more difficult for us.'

The help keeps a towel for Lalita who looks as Mother takes the baby away, blowing on her head, oblivious of her older daughter.

Umabai draws hot water from the copper boiler.

A woman is adding pieces of coconut coir to a copper boiler.

Lalita smiles to herself. So her sister also has her own acts. In Pune, she keeps referring to 'our hometown' and often says, 'Well, I guess, I am just a Konkani girl at heart'. Here, she is the urban, sophisticated advertising professional who looks down on all these silly customs.

As if sensing this, someone pours half a bucket of water on her head.

'Is this cold enough, Vinu baby?' asks the maidservant.

Vinodini looks exasperated.

***

Eleven-year-old Lalita plays in the haud, the water tank. She takes a deep breath and ducks into the water. There is water all around her.

She emerges, obviously having stayed down for as long as she could.

She puts her hands on the edge of the tank and hoists herself up.

Vinodini, three years old, presses her face against the wall of the tank, stands on tiptoe and looks for her sister.

Lalita lifts Vinodini in her arms.

She kisses her sister's cheeks again and again. Lalita is trying to make the child overcome her fear of water.

The child holds on to her sister.

Her arms are around Lalita's neck.

Vinodini shivers.

Lalita hugs her tightly.

***

With the voices of the other people, the light too fades away.

Everything is a little less harsh when they are alone.

The two sisters have just finished their bath. They have only towels wrapped around them. They see themselves reflected in the huge mirror.

They stare at their reflection. Devoid of their usual characteristic clothing, accessories etc, they resemble each other greatly.

Vinodini's confident, sexy image has a lot to do with

the clothes she wears to work.

Now, she is just Lalita's baby sister waiting to see how Akku will react to all that is happening to them, so that she, Vinodini, can know what to feel.

Lalita's frumpy housewife-look has a lot to do with her chosen style of dressing.

Now, she looks very sensuous.

Vinodini puts out a hand and touches a drop of water on Lalita's neck.

Lalita places her left hand on her own heart. With the back of her right hand she touches her sister on the same spot.

They look at each other.

They place their palms together. This is reflected in the mirror.

An image of these two images of one another.

***

There is a hush in the women's conversation as Lalita and Vinodini enter the outer room.

They look clean, fresh and strangely similar.

The men have left for the cremation. The women seem more relaxed now. They are sprawled all over the place. Small groups have formed and conversations continue.

Women catch up with each other, make phone

calls, come out of the kitchen, clearly in the process of preparing a meal, one dozes off, some put their kids to sleep, one feeds her kid.

It is as if the entire house has been taken over.

Lalita and Vinodini sit awkwardly in a corner. They listen to the women's conversation, their gossip and criticism about Mother, disguised as praise.

'It was great the way she managed the hospital.'

Mrs. Borkar's son has ruined whatever Dr. Borkar had put into their eye hospital, hence the management of hospitals is probably on her mind.

Probably, she would like to talk about her hopes for her son, how he might still ably manage it.

But Mrs. Seth will not allow any digression.

'Of course, Dr. Sane was there to help.'

She is quickly rewarded for her presence of mind, for one of the mourner's family joins in the gossip about the dead person. Well, this is going to be good.

'It was the other way around. Dr. Sane's career benefitted because of Ma and our hospital,' mutters Lalita.

Mrs. Borkar and Mrs. Seth smirk at each other.

Mrs. Borkar has forgiven the other woman's taunts made earlier and joined the winning team.

They look as though they are clearly winning, when one says, 'Who helped whom is not important... anyway the poor thing is dead.'

And the other, 'No! No! What is wrong in saying they were "good friends"? She was a working woman unlike us.'

But suddenly, there is a whisper,definitely a whisper but an emphatic one.

'Precisely, Auntie. Being called "doctarin bai" just because you are a doctor's wife, and actually being a doctor are two entirely different identities,' says Lalita. And then, moving closer to Mrs. Seth,

'She was never a poor thing. My mother was a strong woman. You are a poor thing, and every woman in this room knows why.'

Every woman in the room knows why, and Lalita knows how she too is a poor thing because of precisely the same reason as Mrs. Seth is.

She feels sorry for the older woman, but then, she shouldn't have said such things about Mother.

Vinodini is surprised at the way Lalita defends Mother.

Anuradha Auntie pats the space next to her on the sofa. She indicates that Lalita should come and sit next to her.

'You don't come so often nowadays. Your Aphra likes the garden, the lake.'

'My daughter sees her Vinu *Mavshi* in Poona now, ever since Vinu took up that job.'

'So, you used to come to meet only your sister?'

***

'We are going to Ma's house.'

Lalita keeps repeating this as she rocks the baby.

There has been another incident. Lalita does not dwell on the details. It is easier to look forward to the Wadi house.

It is comforting to look forward to being in her childhood home.

Lalita remembers a poem by Bahinabai.

Was it Nakusa who gave it a tune?

A woman sings praises of her maternal home to a traveller.

She tells him to convey her love to her maternal home which he will pass on his travels.

The traveller asks, 'If you love your maternal home so much, why don't you go there?'

And the woman replies, 'I am carrying a child. All the signs say that I am carrying a female child.'

Lekichya maaherasaathi maay saasri naandte.

The Mother lives in her marital home so that she can make a maternal home for her daughter.'

The bus stand is full of people eating, rushing about, finding places to sleep, talking, spitting. There are loud but incomprehensible announcements.

Lalita sits in the midst of all this and breast-feeds the baby.

Lalita sees a man looking at her, adjusts her own clothes and covers the baby's legs too.

The man continues to look at her.

He can see her through the glass, pleading on the phone. She taps the phone. Will he know that the person on the other end has hung up? Does this allow him to continue looking?

Not only is she not accompanied by her husband, but he obviously does not even want to talk to her on the phone.

An unwanted woman.

Is that why she can be wanted by other men, looked at by them?

Lalita comes out of the booth and counts her money.

She looks at a stall with soft drink bottles.

She walks on.

People look at her as she makes her way out, baby in the sling, a bag overflowing with the usual baby's things.

Lalita sits on a concrete bench. Something is physically hurting her. She looks down at her feet. She takes off her chappals

Lalita's feet are swollen from the journey. Her chappals do not fit.

She had bought these chappals at this very bus stop, the last time she visited Mother.

Kolhapuri chappals.

Kolhapur bus stand.

Right in the middle of the journey from Mahesh's home and Mother's home.

A good place wherefrom to call both these homes and find out whether she was needed at either.

A good place.

The goddess' place.

Zaid's joke about the place.

About how people took the literal meaning of words unlike Lalita who was crazy enough to look for other meanings.

'Kolhapurchi Ambabai, tu mala pav,' would be translated as Fox flood mango lady, you me bread.

The actual meaning of course was,

'Goddess Ambabai of Kolhapur, please bless me.'

Ambabai, the fierce but kind Mother goddess.

Mother.

Where was Zaid now? This was his second posting in the government health services. Which unwanted, faraway place had he chosen this time?

'We are going to Ma's house,' she tells her one-year-old Aphra.

Aphra needs milk from Mamma's breast.

Mamma needs to drink something.

Mamma has run off from home with just her vegetable-money purse, has bought a ticket and has no money to buy something to drink.

Mamma sees another woman drinking water from a tap.

Lalita walks with a shuffling gait because she has to drag her chappals. Lalita reaches the water tap with her infant daughter. She is bent over a basin, trying to wash the baby.

She looks down and sees how the sink is clogged and there are old food particles (vomit?) floating in the water. Nauseated, she turns the baby away from it.

She will clean her baby, powder it, make her doll smell pretty.

Her one pretty thing in a nauseating world.

It is dinnertime for the bus and all the other passengers have gone down to the restaurant. A popular song blares in the distance, there is laughter, and people call out to each other. Sounds of noisy throats clearing, reversing tunes and loud growls of starting buses fill the air.

The red bus is parked in a narrow space between two other buses.

Alone with Mamma at last, Aphra begins to cry.

Inside, the green walls, lit by one yellow and one blue overhead bulb seem to converge. In an even narrower space, Lalita lays down the baby on the dark seat, and undoes the sling.

She touches the baby's thigh – there is a weal on it where the buckle has probably hurt the baby – Lalita kisses it, and starts crying.

Mamma rocks the baby muttering words to it, hopefully in a tone which does not betray how displaced she feels.

'Green walls lit by one blue bulb and one yellow bulb.'

A red water flask with a plastic glass has been kept near the wall that separates the driver's cabin from the passengers.

The trickle from the tap is very slow. Lalita lifts the lid, dips the glass in and drinks.

Mahesh is probably having his whisky on the rocks in one of the new glasses she bought yesterday.

His friends are probably with him and have helped him forget that his wife has fled to her mother's house because he hit her too badly this time.

I will be okay, she tells herself, we will soon reach Mother's house. Now that she has found water, she will no longer be parched and she will be able to feed her baby.

Lalita holds the baby close to her. Both mother and child relax a little as the milk begins to flow.

The motion of the bus, once they resume the journey, makes the baby sleepy. Lalita, her head resting against the bars of the window, looks out. It is dark. Far away, she can see a few houses illuminated by lamps.It is a tribal hamlet.

Male vocal rendition of Raga Pooriya Dhanashree. What was the name of that singer? She asks her reflection in the window ahead of her seat.

What was the name of the singer?

She looks out of the window again.

A Bharadwaj bird flies away.

Birds don't fly about at night.

Yearning is not supposed to make a face more beautiful.

***

Lalita's face reflected on the glass of an old photograph. It is one of the parents in happier times. She wipes the dust off the surface.

'Lost as usual in making up a fantasy,' Vinodini looks down upon her sister yet again.

Back in the other room, the way Akku had spoken to those women – was she the same woman?

'Lost as usual in making up a fantasy...' says Vinodini as she passes Lalita on the way outside to get a clearer signal on her phone.

She does not even wait to hear Lalita respond.

Lalita does not want to say anything.

Lalita wishes she could just hold her baby sister. There was a moment when she could have,when Vinodini passed her on her way outside.

But the moment had passed.

'...to help me through reality.'

Lalita wishes she could just bundle Vinu into a *chaadar* and hold her tight, as she had done when they were little.

Saying something to hurt her Akku and then running away was an old habit.

'Don't sit calling out to her. Be a *junglee*.' Khala had taught her how to put a bed sheet over 'that wild sister' of hers and trap her.

'That should scare the rudeness out of her.'

It didn't, for the little brat loved it.

She then wanted to be cradled in the sheet, Zaid Dada and Akku holding it on both sides, and ABBA songs playing on the tape recorder.

Mamma Mia, here I go again.

Vinodini looks at Lalita touching Mother's face in the photograph.

'Sometimes it seems that you really loved her.'

'Of course I did, Vinu. Only, I did not place her on a pedestal like you did.'

Vinu reminds herself of the fights between her sister and Mother. 'You were always critical of her. Always analysing.'

'And why is that bad?' asks Lalita. 'When you are sure of a love, you are not afraid to demystify,' she tells Vinodini.

'LOVE.' Vinodini scoffs at her.

'Everyone seems to have an opinion on it.'

Attya overhears only this part of the conversation.

'When is Vinodini planning to get married?'

Vinodini stops just for a moment and looks at Lalita.

'Hello. Yeah, there's too much noise here Nikhil; you'll hear me when I step out...'

She leaves her sister to deal with that pest of a lady and goes out.

'I hope you are not going to start your usual speech. I cannot believe this. You sound so much like Lalita.'

'Yeah', laughs Nikhil, 'We do have a lot in common. I only try for the younger sister because I can never get the one I really want.'

***

Vinodini looks at a swing tied to the mango tree and smiles.

'I won't let you fall. Hold on tightly.' says Lalita.

Vinodini sits on it and starts swinging.

'I'll fall, I'll tumble down —

I'll break my head —

I'll make Akku cry.'

Vinodini holds the rope tighter.

'I won't let you fall. Hold on tightly.'

Lalita was just twelve when she had said that, when she was protector, even Mother to her four-year-old sister.

Why had she not held on tighter when it came to herself? Why did she give in? This garden has been a witness to it.

Uncared for, unkempt now.

Like an old dog-eared book still holding the scenes of a story.

***

Mango leaves, marigold flowers and lamps decorate the courtyard. A wedding has been conducted a little while ago. Vinodini holds the rope of the swing, their swing.

'Enough now.' Mother had said and the teenager had brought the swing to a sudden halt.

The ditch under the swing that accumulates water in the rainy season; has it been the result of many such sudden halts?

'It is better that you return to college tomorrow, or are you also planning to let me down?' Why is mother so disappointed, the fourteen-year-old had wondered. Hadn't Akku agreed to an arranged marriage with this doctor from the city?

Akku did not look happy either. Shouldn't she be glad Mamma had allowed her to marry a doctor if not actually become one herself?

Lalita had wanted to become a doctor. She had secured good marks in the twelfth board exam but had then shifted to the Arts stream for her BA.

Mother had said that becoming a doctor was part of her plan to become a Muslim and she would never allow that. Vinodini had wondered what the connection had been.

Zaid Dada would have been able to tell her but suddenly, he had stopped coming over.

Akku had wanted to study. Akku had not wanted to marry this doctor called Gune from Pune.

Mamma said that People would say that just because Dr. Patwardhan had died, Mother had not been able to control Akku.

That should never be allowed to happen, Vinodini had decided as she saw her Mamma cry.

Akku was so bad, so ungrateful. How could she make Mamma cry after all that she had done for them?

After Baba died in an accident.

To make Mamma sadder, he had been on his way to meet another woman when his car had caught fire.

No more crying for Nalini Patwardhan.

People should never say that she had not been able to 'control' Akku. What did control mean?

Vinu would help her mother in whatever it was.

Baba had made Mamma cry.

Akku was not to be allowed to make Mamma cry.

Some mourners cry loudly near Mother's framed photograph.

Vinodini switches off the phone and walks towards the door.

***

Fourteen year old Vinodini reaches home after school. She looks at the window. She seems surprised that Mother is not at the window waiting as usual. She walks through the dark house looking for Mother.

Whenever she has needed a mother, she has walked like this, looking for her Akku.

Today, Mother needs her.

How can Akku dare to want something that will embarrass her Mother?

Hasn't Mother been embarrassed enough?

There are fights between Mamma and Akku now.

Just like those other fights.

And although it makes Vinodini sad that Akku's head was banged against the wall yesterday, she knows which side she should be on.

Mamma will never be left alone, now, the way she was left alone by Father.

Mother is sitting by the kitchen platform. She tells Vinodini something. She appears hurt. It is apparent that she is complaining about Lalita. Vinodini looks angrily at the door.

Mother rubs her chest with a closed fist.

What if she gets those heart pains again?

What if she dies?

What if she too, dies?

Vinodini picks up the big iron pestle in the corner.

She marches into the room she shares with her sister. Lalita is lying on the floor reading a copy of Great Expectations. She looks up at Vinodini and smiles.

***

Lalita looks up at Vinodini and smiles.

She has obviously been trying to defend Vinodini from Attya's intrusive question.

'When is Vinodini planning to get married?'

'The only plan I have now is to sell this house and start my own advertising firm.'

She knows what Lalita will do next. She will tell Vinodini that she agrees with Attya, she should think of getting married.

Vinodini will know that she is doing this only out of respect for Attya. She is, after all, their father's sister.

She will subject Vinodini to this kind of ridiculous conversation only to tell Attya that it was okay to bring this up, that Attya was not violating an adult woman's space.

Lalita will say things that she herself does not believe in, simply to reassure Attya, to allow Attya to keep her dignity.

She will do this taking Vinodini's understanding and complicity for granted.

But Vinodini is fed up.

'Please. No lectures. I don't think anyone is an authority on marriages here.'

This will shut her up, Vinodini knows for she herself is quite an authority on Lalita's marriage. So is Attya, so is everybody that Nalini has expressed her disappointment to.

Yes, this will shut her up.

***

Yes, Lalita is no expert on marriages.

Experts say that certain kind of women take such shit from men simply because they have no will, no strength to get out of the status quo.

Experts write about the reason for divorce.

Experts write about the causes of break-ups.

Can there be reasons for stay-ons too?

What are the reasons that a woman might choose to stay on in a marriage?

Lalita looks at Mahesh. What could be the reasons?

The reason lies not with this man but with someone who he is arguing with on the telephone.

He will lose the argument.

He will look at his wife and smile.

Her daughter has something that Lalita lost at around the age Aphra is at now.

Aphra is arguing with her father.

And winning.

Will this help the other arguments in her life?

Other relationships?

Do you learn to stand up to your husband if you have argued with your father?

What do experts have to say about that?

And about the confidence that a woman gets just knowing that there is a family she can always go back to?

Lekichya maaherasaathi maay saasri naandte.

The mother stays on in her marital home, so that her daughter can have a maternal home.

This is not to say that a woman should bear pain, take insults, simply for the sake of her daughter.

All of us have our reasons; this was Lalita's.

This is not to say that it is reason enough.

This is not to say that experts are wrong either.

Experts' work is important. For example, the connections they make between victims of domestic violence and childhood violence.

Lalita's face is devoid of any expression so that Vinodini can believe that she has indeed made her shut up.

Vinodini.

Lalita's hand goes to her own back.

***

Vinodini is afraid that Lalita will kill her mother.

Hasn't Mother said that Lalita's behaviour will kill her one day?

What has Akku done now?, Vinodini wonders.

What if Mamma gets those heart pains again?

What if she dies?

What if she too, dies?

Vinodini is fourteen years old and this is her greatest fear.

Her Vinu used to be afraid of the dark, Lalita remembers.

The bulbs begin to flicker when there is an impending power failure.

Her baby sister is a big girl now. She is no longer scared of the dark.

However, out of habit, Lalita puts down Great Expectations, and calls out,

'Vinu! Come here.'

Vinodini walks up to Lalita.

She brings down the pestle on her sister's back.

The lights go out.

***

Lalita is walking in the totally dark house.

The twenty-two-year-old knows this house although she hasn't come here in a long time.

She reaches the lone source of light.

A glow of light filters from a room.

Thirt-four year old Lalita walks into the library. She looks at his wide brow from where she stands. At thirty-eight, his hairline is already receding, he will look like Karim Uncle soon.

Zaid squats down in front of a bookcase. An old copy of the *Oxford Textbook of Psychiatry* lies on the floor. Zaid is unaware that Lalita watches him.

Lalita, twenty-two years old, asks her best friend 'If I die, will I go to Baba?'

Zaid, twenty-six years of age, is shocked. He makes her sit at the table. He gets down a copy of the Oxford Textbook of Psychiatry. He finds a page.

'Suicidal thoughts and ideas that death could unite them with the lost parent — Stress following the suicide of a parent is the most intense of all types of bereavement.'

Lalita closes the book.

'Chronic grief — you have already discussed it with me Doctor sahaab or is it still Mr. Medical student?'

'Then, why do you continue talking like an idiot?'

Zaid, now thirty-eight years old, opens various drawers in the light of his cigarette lighter.

'Those who survive other people's suicides need special "postvention" help.'

Zaid continues, holding her hand which she has kept over the closed book.

Zaid finds a candle and stands up.

'Schneidman-1973' she says. The thirty-four-year-old woman remembers how somebody had cared enough for her, had been concerned about what happened to her, and had dealt it with the only way he knew – by trying to find answers in his books.

There was more that Zaid had offered and she had not been able to accept.

Lalita closes her eyes as Zaid touches his cheek to hers. He whispers in her ear.

'Our secret...,' she says now that years have passed.

'...that I wanted someone to know,' he reminds her.

'A dream that you would "rescue" me,' she admits, several years too late.

He holds the lighter in front of her face. So close, that she moves back afraid, she has after all wronged him so terribly.

'For a rescue, first an invasion is needed. Would you have allowed me to breach her world in any way?'

The flame is extinguished.

She is comforted to know that he too has been reading Great Expectations. There is a copy on his table. It is as if he was with her when she was hurt. It is not even necessary to tell him that Vinodini hit her with a stone pestle.

***

She has run to Khala's house to tell her that she is hurt, Khala will make it go away. But Khala is dead.

She lifts up her kurta and shows him the bruise. He places both his hands on either side of her spine.

She wants him to place his mouth on the bruise. She wants him to hold her.

She does not want to resist.

He remembers her resistance.

She remembers her resistance, and wants him to have forgotten it.

He remembers a twenty-year old boy's feeling of being rejected.

He removes his hands from her back.

He pulls her kurta down and covers her properly.

She closes her eyes. He has not forgotten. And she will remember this forever.

It would be easy to repent a certain gesture of rejection towards a person whom one actually loved. But what Lalita had felt could not be redeemed, rightly so, for she had felt an acute revulsion.

She knows now that there can be no balm for him, perhaps because of what she had gone through to feel that way.

Whatever the reason was, she had lost him.

She would be punished for that momentary revulsion with a lifetime of hopeless love.

When her eyes open, he is already seated at the table.

Lalita looks at Zaid's beautiful hands as he lights a candle, holds the lit candle in his hand. On the table are a wati or a small bowl of water and the copy of Great Expectations.

She is not alone. He will always be with her.

And yet, she knows that she has ruined her chance of having a life with him.

A lifetime of hopeless love.

He is creating a pattern in the water by letting the wax drip bit by bit.

Lalita and Zaid look at each other.

'Do it,' she says, and he turns the wati over.

The water flows away to leave a beautiful patterned sheet of wax.

Zaid places it in Lalita's hand.

Almost a decade has gone by.

His face is darker now, because of the beard, more because of his hard life as a surgeon in a difficult area.

But his hands are the same.

Hands that she had loved, hands that she had rejected.

Momentary revulsion.

And a lifetime of hopeless love.

'It's time you learnt to take what's yours,' he says now.

He closes her fingers over the wax pattern he has made.

***

Lalita's fingers are tightly curled around a branch of the chikoo tree.

'Nandita.' she whispers and rests her forehead on the branch.

Vinodini switches off her cell phone when she notices that she is not alone. She points to a branch, smiling,'Akku, you used to sit there and talk to your imaginary friend.'

Lalita looks up at the girl sitting on the tree, her long legs hanging on either side of the branch.

In the years that they have not met, the imagined Nandita has acquired a little of Aphra's personality, Lalita smiles to herself, the way she's dangling those long legs.

Her face though is unchanged. She's still a strange combination of Lalita and Vinu.

'Not friend.'

Lalita peeps through a window into the parents' room. Mother lies on her back, with her knees folded up. A nurse gives Mother an injection on her thigh. Father checks her pulse.

Mother's white thighs are spread open — so that is where babies come from.

She herself has not come out of an expanding umbilicus as she had assumed, it seemed a likely exit for a baby.

Lalita has come out from that secret part of Mamma's body.

Mother lifts herself up slightly and a blood string stretches between her bottom and the bed.

Mother's petticoat with a new red patch.

New? It wasn't there when she saw Mamma come out of the bathroom in her petticoat and blouse this morning.

The blood has now dried up.

Mother's petticoat with the new–old red patch has been pulled up almost to her chest.

Under the bed in an enamel bowl, Lalita sees some cotton fully soaked with blood.

Umabai's large bottom with the pleats of her nine yard saree dividing it, making it even larger, has been introduced into Lalita's line of vision to make her laugh. It does not work. The child is angry that Umabai has blocked her view and sad that she has lost someone she was waiting for.

Lalita sits down. Her old baby toys are all nicely arranged around her.

She chooses a silver rattle.

The servant has dug a hole under the tree. She mutters to herself. Lalita watches.

The child looks at the open enamel bowl kept on the ground next to the hole.

I must not look at it again, Lalita decides then. She wants to erase it from her mind right away.

But the hurting thing in the enamel bowl has felt the anguish in the child's mind.

And like all beings who are themselves hurting, it settles in, content in the thought that long after it has been buried, has rotted in earth, this hurt will always be alive in Lalita's mind.

The seven-year-old girl has not lost someone she was waiting for. Someone who was waiting for her has found her.

Lalita cries loudly, her hair all over her face.

'Stop that noise. Let me bury this properly. If the dogs catch the smell they will dig it up and eat it.'

The child's cries are louder.

She puts her hands on Umabai's shoulders and shakes her.

'It It It It, what do you mean It?'

Thinking of it as It helps take harsh life-saving decisions.

Umabai hopes that Lalita will never know those.

She likes this child but now, Umabai is angry at the child's outburst, she has work to do.

'Her name is Nandita,' Lalita howls, her hair all over her face.

She throws the silver rattle in.

The first layers of mud have already been put back into the hole. How will Nandita reach the toy?

The buried thing has not yet grown hands.

Lalita's hands begin to dig.

'Stop it. Do you want the ghost to come and haunt you?'

Ghosts are scary people.

This was Nandita: she was going to be Lalita's baby sister.

Umabai puts in the final layers of earth and then lays stones over the mound.

It cannot get out, thank god; what if Umabai's threat about being haunted was true?

It would have been Nandita.

It is buried. Nandita is buried.

The child looks bewildered.

A long tendril of hair keeps getting into her eye.

***

Vinodini pushes back a stray strand of hair from Lalita's face.

'This is where you brought me for my birthday gifts- after Mamma had given her big expensive present and before my friends came with inexpensive hair clips, you said and taught me to see it, the present you thought I should have, the present which you made in your head.'

'Did you really see them Vinu, or did you just humour your Akku?'

'I saw how you knew what I really wanted.'

'I never had any pocket money, never thought of asking for some to buy you a present. It was always too late anyway. I would spend a whole week beautifying, embellishing the made-up thing and by the time your birthday actually dawned I would be too exhausted to do anything.'

'Akku, I always liked your imaginary gifts more than the real ones I got from others because they had your dreams attached to them.'

'Aphra will need some real gifts now.' Lalita is exhausted again, but this time she won't let it be too late.

'So? Her successful cardiologist father will provide, I'm sure.'

'You were right you know, Vinu. What do I do just sitting around at home? As Aphra is growing up, I realise how I should have had a proper job, some money of my own.'

Vinodini is wary now.

'You should have thought of this before when you used to say how you wanted to be a "proper mother". Now, if you're trying to say that Mom's money...'

'Vinu, please don't talk to me like that.'

'You should have talked to her about your future plans. You could have told her if you needed any help. The way I told her that I wanted to start my own ad agency.'

'When did all this talk take place? Whenever she was very ill and I was caring for her, you never seemed to be here. When I suggested we should all come and stay together in the old house, you were too busy.'

'I came here a fortnight ago,' admits Vinodini.

'And conspired behind my back.' Lalita hugs a horizontal branch.

'Anyway, it does not make a difference. You do not *have* any plan. Do you, Akku?'

Lalita is very angry. She hugs the branch even closer.

'Get away from MY tree!' she screams.

Vinodini looks shocked. Lalita has never spoken to her like this. Lalita makes an effort to control herself. Vinodini will go away, her sister knows that look. Lalita goes close to her sister. She caresses Vinodini's head urgently, trying to repeat a touch that once worked.

'Nandita and Baba are here. Now, Ma is also here. How can we give the house to someone else *beta*?'

Vinodini pushes away her hand. She looks at Lalita. Lalita has a strange expression on her face—a blend of loss and anger.

A facial expression is strange when other people find it inappropriate or just unusual.

To a close one however, this strange expression brings with it a reminder of its past appearances, one's own past reactions to it.

The expression also appears to show the irony of it being so unusual, even rare because it in fact defines the person, the relationship too well.

Lalita has always been lost and angry.

Vinodini has always been a little afraid of her and has always felt an extreme love for her sister.

If she holds Lalita, if she allows the love, the agency, the ambition will have to be given up.

Everything that is controllable will end.

Love will destroy control.

And now that Mother is gone, isn't it all the more necessary to sustain the control?

Isn't it up to Vinodini to sustain it? Yes, she will. Yes, she can for there is always the anger.

Just one look at this useless, helpless failure of a sister and the way she spoke to her as if they were still children.

Exercising the only superiority that she can claim over Vinodini with the eight-year age difference between them.

'Nandita and Baba are here. Now, Ma is also here. How can we give the house to someone else *beta*?'

'You are totally out of your mind, Lalita. You always have been.'

'And you are sane to let them blast our childhood home, just for some money?' Lalita holds her sister's shoulder. She wants Vinodini to look at her Akku. Will she be able to call her by name even then?

The stronger Vinodini moves away from her quickly.

'Everybody is doing it,' she says.

'And raping the town — you want to join them?'

She puts her hand on a plant stem to stop herself from hitting this stranger who seems to have no understanding of what their family, the town means to both of them.

She looks at the hibiscus plant. In the city there are new varieties, so many new kinds that this one — the old ordinary red shoe flower has become rare.

'You used to give B-complex injections to these if you thought they "looked ill", Vinu. I collected them from the dustbin so that you could imagine you were making a difference, when you weren't, you couldn't. Now when you can make a difference, you seem to have gone far away from the land. Do whatever you want. Maybe you have your own reasons for wanting to give up something so precious.'

Lalita walks off. She keeps walking even beyond the house. Vinodini sees her go out of the gate.

***

Lalita walks along the wall of the school compound. The old stone school building has clearly been recently joined by a rather loud new concrete construction. She stands on tiptoe and looks inside. It is recess time. Children sit under trees with their tiffin boxes. An older girl takes out a lunch box from a bag and gives it to her younger sister. The younger child takes it and runs away. The older one, water bottle in hand, calls after her.

The younger child slips out of the small, rotating

gate close to where Lalita stands. The older sister sees Lalita as she calls out. They smile at each other and shrug their shoulders.

Lalita sees children buying local soft drinks at a shop. She walks into a lane adjacent to it.

An old house is being blasted. Workmen break down walls. An ornate door is thrown on a rubbish heap. Rubble lies all around.

Broken pieces of an old earthen pot.

Lalita dips a tumbler into an earthen pot and pours water for the others. A big tray of cut raw mango is kept beside the pot. Lalita surreptitiously pockets some. The woman of the house comes out. The girls run. The woman calls out to Lalita and gives her some jaggery.

'Share it with those monkeys,' says she.

Her house is near the school. The girls go there in the lunch break to drink water. There is an earthen pot full of cool water for the girls. A wet white cloth is wrapped around it.

Mother has forbidden Lalita to go and drink water from this house, we don't know who the people are, what caste…

The girls like Lalita to accompany them to the house. There is always a piece of jaggery for the doctor's child, and for the girls with her.

So Lalita goes, dreading the moment when she will be reminded that she is breaking a rule, for the lady will ask 'Aai kashi aahe ga, how is Mother?'

Where is that lady now?

Did she die here alone, after her children migrated to Mumbai? Where did the thirsty girls go then?

Or, did she go and live in her son's small flat? And did she wonder why there were no thirsty girls in the city?

A man tells Lalita to get out of the way. He throws a load of broken *chira*, the local red brick, pieces right next to where Lalita stands. The dust gets into her eyes. She walks out of the compound.

Lalita walks through the town.

New shops — garish signs of the kind of unplanned development one sees in our small towns.

Contrasting, often ridiculous pictures depicting this. She looks at everything, but does not want to make eye contact with anyone. If there is even a flicker of recognition on a face, she quickly walks away. Lalita traverses the market and crowded areas to come to a quieter part of the town. She reaches the gate of Mother's house. Vinodini stands on the verandah and sees Lalita enter the garden.

Lalita touches the gate. She presses her hand on the pointed bars.

***

Lalita is twelve years old. She clings on to the gate. Mother tries to make her get into a car. The family in the car too tries to coax her. Another family, her own, is not coming with her.

'Your mother needs some rest Lalita. Now get into the car. I want to reach the school by two.' says Uncle.

Rest from what? 'Mamma, you cannot send me away from my Vinu.'

On the steps of the house, Vinu who is now four years old puts her head on her knees and sobs.

'I will not go.' screams Lalita, she has to hug her sister, make her stop crying.

She clings on even tighter. Mother starts walking towards the house, not looking at the child. Uncle disengages her hands forcibly. He opens the door of the car. He starts pushing her into the car.

'Just because you were asked whether you wanted to go, did you imagine that you really had a choice?'

Lalita calls out to her mother.

'Mamma, you lied to me.'

A holiday in Bombay, watching an English movie in a cool theatre, and eating a chocobar icecream was not what this was about. This was Mama and Mami, her Uncle and Aunt driving her to Panchgani, to a boarding school. Somebody had packed her things in a trunk. How would they have known what she needed to take with her? And Mamma, who would rest if Lalita was sent away?

'Mamma, you lied to me.'

So, mothers lie.

Lalita looks at Mother as she goes to her four-year-old on the steps. Mother tries to make Vinodini lift up her head. Vinodini runs towards her sister.

Vinodini walks towards the gate.

'It was you who wanted to go to the boarding school, nobody forced you to. You used to read all those Enid Blyton school stories — Mallory Towers, St.Clare's and what not.'

One of her sudden statements which could have been better understood if she at least had some expression on her face, thinks Lalita. Although Vinodini is her pretty, fair baby sister, she had often felt that her face could do with some colour.

'Did it occur to you that so many were suddenly bought for me that summer?' says she now even as she remembers how she would actually draw on Vinodini's face.

Does Vinodini not remember those drawing sessions? The particular one that Lalita recollects just now?

Was she too small to hear that conversation between Mother and Anuradha Auntie?

Or is she too far away to remember it now?

Twelve-year-old Lalita paints Vinodini's face. The younger child is chirping away happily. Suddenly Lalita hushes her up. She looks at Mother and Anuradha Auntie as they sip tea.

'*...and so are the tantrums. I just want to concentrate on Vinodini now. This one irritates me, she is so much like him.*'

'*Your daughter will "straighten up" after going off to hostel.*'

'Do you want to pick your daughter up before going to Nasik?' Vinodini wants to know.

'Aphra. Her name is Aphra.'

'We are leaving tomorrow morning. I have a lot of stuff to do before that. I need to know. We could stop at your house in Pune and take her with us.'

'Yes, we should. It's been more than a week. She's never stayed without me for so long.'

'But she's with Audrey, isn't she? Why do you want her to miss school? And she can stay alone — she's not a baby now.'

'In fact, this is a terrible age to be alone.'

'Still stuck on the boarding school thing. Not everyone has the luxury of blaming everything on the past and making excuses. You seem to have all the time for that.'

'If you had to learn to use sanitary napkins from a warden, a complete stranger, you too would make the time.'

Any woman who did not have her mother by her

side when she got her first period knows how cruel it is to be alone.

All women have tales about the day they first saw a red stain on their underwear. It could be anything ranging from 'I thought I was dying' to 'of course, I had heard about it, knew what it was, but to feel that hot sticky fluid come out of my own body – Yucks.' But the line that follows all this is common to most- 'then Mother came'.

Mother came, Mother said, Mother gave, Mother made, Mother applied, Mother held, Mother was there.

For some girls, however, Mother was not there.

The Mother who was not there is not to be blamed for she did not consciously choose to stay away.

Maybe Mother was not there because she was worried about her marriage which did not seem to be going so well in it's thirteenth year.

Maybe Mother was busy earning her living.

Or perhaps she thought her life had passed by, for surely now with her child becoming a woman, wasn't she getting old?

Mother's mind was occupied with something other than her daughter.

It is not her fault, but the result is that her daughter had a lonely menarche.

And she will have a lonely childbirth.

When she delivers her first child, she will still feel Mother's absence. Although things will be more settled then, and the Mother may have time to spend with the new mother, yet the years will have taken their toll.

How can she suddenly get close to a woman who once wasn't there?

In contrast, there are some women who have Mother with them even at menopause.

Although they might be so old, that their Mother would have died by then.

They are confident, strong, cared for. Not because somebody is mothering them now when they are fifty, but because on that day, when they were fifteen, she had loved them.

Mother had come, Mother had said, Mother had given, Mother had made, Mother had applied, Mother had held, Mother had been there.

Some will understand that she couldn't be there and will learn to fend for themselves.

Lalita who has heard Mother telling Anuradha Auntie 'I don't know how to tell her about chumming, frankly, I don't want to. Just one look at her sorry face and...' will never learn. What was chumming, she had wondered and then found out at boarding school.

To know that mother couldn't be bothered enough.

To feel abandoned forever.

To feel alone.

But had she really been alone in that abandoned state, she looks at Vinodini now.

'If I'm the one who dwells in the past, how did you know that I was thinking about the time I was sent off to the boarding school, Vinu?'

Vinodini looks at the gate.

Four year old Vinodini presses her face between the bars of the gate.

'Akku!' she calls out.

***

'Come.' Lalita says.

She holds the sleeve of Vinodini's shirt.

They walk into a consulting room, built as an extension to the house.

Lalita opens an old cupboard. She runs a hand along the spines of old surgery texts.

'Only you came into his consulting room,' complains Vinodini. 'It was too painful for her she said. And to me it never had any meaning.'

Lalita puts the stethoscope to her ears. She keeps its diaphragm on her own chest.

Heartbeats.

A male vocal rendition of the Raga *Pooriya Dhanashri*.

And heartbeats.

Lalita enters a tribal village. She drives through it in a white jeep ,the kind one sees in primary health centres. The only sources of light are the lamps inside the houses — women wash dishes outside, a few men smoke bidis and talk. She is greeted by the villagers. She seems not to know what she is doing here. The jeep stops outside a hut, which is quite like the other huts in the village, but has been modified into a clinic. Petromax lamps make this place slightly brighter than the rest of the village.

There are a few patients waiting on benches. They greet her. The compounder also seems happy to see her.

Lalita walks into the examination room.

Baba is examining a patient. He gets up and holds out his arms.

Lalita runs and hugs him.

'I never believed them Baba.'

She is very happy. She puts her head on his chest.

Her hand goes to his shirt pocket,she looks at his usual pen,and then sees a yellow envelope. She pulls it out of the pocket partly,puts it back. She is shocked.

Lalita looks up at father's face — he is crying. She breaks free and runs out.

The hut is empty except for dried leaves. She keeps running, the houses are dark and empty. Tears stream down her face.

Tears stream down Lalita's face. She keeps the stethoscope away.

'Dreaming again?' Vinodini is a little fed up of this and just wants to be back in her flat in Pune. She does not want to be in any of these old rooms.

'Baba's dream, Vinu.'

Vinodini touches some circles drawn in crayon. A map of Maharashtra hangs on the wall. Circles have been drawn around some tribal areas.

'He wanted to drag all of us to some god forsaken place.'

Lalita also puts her hand on the same map.

'When we planned all this – he and me,' she smiles as she notices how she sounds. She is an adult pretending to be a child who is pretending to be an adult —'Baba and I planned this', 'Baba and I decided'.

'When Baba and I talked about it, he told me that there was no English-medium school there.'

'Thank god for Mum. Just imagine.' Vinodini shudders. As it is, having been educated at an English-medium school but one in the Konkan, she has to be very careful with her pronunciations to avoid that question she was often asked in her early advertising days: "Are you from a vernac school?"'

'I was in the fifth standard then.' Lalita retains the accent, she had more friends from the Marathi-medium schools. Vinodini remembers Mother's exasperation at Lalita's friends — all poor children and it seemed like Lalita deliberately chose her friends to embarrass Mother.

She does that with language too, deliberately emphasises the Marathi accent. Vinodini has noticed that the richer, more urbane, more sophisticated the company is, sharper does Lalita's *Marathipana* become.

Yet, despite this, her sister sounds more natural than her and after listening to Americanisms at office, listening to Lalita is, although she will never say that, like coming home.

'I was in the fifth standard then and he was worried whether I could cope with the change in language. And I said, "As long as Vinu and I are together."'

'You have all these memories of him — I was just two years old when he died, Akku.'

'But you had all of Mamma.'

'She was All I had.'

Maybe Mother wanted to be all Vinodini had; maybe that is why she was always torn away from her Akka.

Vinodini looks at her as if she knows what is going to follow.

Thankfully, her cell phone rings out her funny sms tone which somehow seems macabre in the present situation.

And of course big sister is looking at her disapprovingly. What did she expect, that Vinodini would have had the time to change her ring tones for the occasion, as soon as Mother died?

Yes, Mother had died, and there were important things to be done.

She will not allow Lalita to drag her into this memory thing.

She reads the text message and tells Lalita.

'I have to go and sign some papers for Mr. Kanvinde at eleven today.'

Lalita sees how her sister does not look at her as she says this, as she leaves the room.

She should not drag Vinodini into what she probably calls a 'memory thing', she should not bother her baby sister with all this.

What had the whole conversation been about anyway?

Was the discussion about the Marathi-medium school in some tribal area?

'As it turned out we never did speak the same language.'

Lalita comes out of the consulting room. She latches the door.

Vinodini comes back to the door.

'This is what happens. I always forget what I have to really ask you.'

'Yes. I will take Aphra along.'

'Then I'd better tell them. Shriram Bhatji said that we'll leave early tomorrow.'

Suddenly, Lalita looks pale.

'Vinu, lets not take her. School is starting in a few days and...'

Vinodini is exasperated — this kind of indecision is typical of Lalita.

Also typical is this look: even after upsetting people's plans, leaving them confused, Lalita looks as though she is the one upset, as if being called upon to make a simple decision is an attack.

Vinodini walks away.

Lalita looks at her, wants her to wait, to listen.

A stream of sweat trickles from her neck into her bra.

She wishes she could take this saree off.

***

Lalita, twelve years old, is dressed in a saree, sitting cross-legged on a paat, a wooden platform seat, with the priest. A pooja, a religious ceremony, is being performed. Mother looks on.

Shriram Bhatji presses tulsi leaves and flowers into Lalita's hand.

He holds her wrist tightly.

He indicates that she should open her fist.

He puts teerth, the holy water, into her hand.

She drinks it.

This is repeated thrice.

A little water on Lalita's lips.

A vermilion mark with rice grains on her forehead. Some of this mixture of red kumkum and rice grains has spilt on her chest.

Shriram Bhatji stands with a glass in his hand.

He wipes his mouth after taking a gulp of milk. Mother directs Lalita to touch his feet.

The priest blesses the child.

His hand presses her shoulder.

He looks at the little girl.

As Lalita comes to her Mother's room, she pulls the saree off her body.

He looked at this: she yanks it off.

The safety pin on her shoulder tears the expensive silk.

His eyes lingered on this blouse: she rips it open, the buttons fall off.

The safety pin has already torn the blouse too.

The safety pin on her shoulder.

His hand has pressed this shoulder.

As she rubs an antiseptic soap on her shoulder, she opens and shuts her legs inside the water tank that she is standing in.

Open shut and open shut and feel clean if you can.

Open shut and open shut and feel clean if you can.

Get 'Unlooked at' again.

As unblessed as you can.

Unblessed enough to curse.

To fight.

'Mamma, if such a pooja is held when Vinu grows up, I'm going to kill that man.'

Lalita barges into mother's room wearing trousers and a tee-shirt. Mother is reading a magazine. The girls in the magazines are pretty and curvy. They seem to like being looked at.

As unlooked as you can.

Mother looks up.

'Bhatji said..'

'Why did you have to tell him Mamma?'

'Bhatji said we had to have the ceremony because you got your first menses on an inauspicious day.'

'I don't want that man to have anything to do with my sister. Nothing about Vinodini's life is ever going to be inauspicious.'

Contrary to their characteristic relationship, Mother seems actually afraid of her.

Lalita walks out of the door.

***

Lalita, now thirty-four, comes out on the porch.

'God willing, the next time we meet, it will be an auspicious occasion,' says Mrs. Seth.

The women take leave of Vinodini.

Ms. Vinodini Patwardhan folds her hand in a *namaskar*. She is gracious, even elegant. Like Mother.

Lalita is not interested.

She stares at the urn containing Mother's ashes.

Mrs. Borkar looks at Mrs. Seth as if to indicate that Lalita has always been ungracious as compared to her sister.

'I cannot believe that two girls with the same upbringing can be so different.'

Lalita turns around sharply to look at Mrs. Khadilkar.

The little girl scowls at Mrs. Khadilkar.

'I cannot believe that this place is so untidy,' she has just said.

About Mamma's house.

Their house.

The same women, much younger, are looking for appropriate white clothes to dress Lalita in. They go about using this opportunity to peek into cupboards, rummage through drawers, and so on.

'She must be too busy to tidy the house.'

'When I see such houses, I'm so happy I don't have a job

you know. Doctor Borkar likes the house to be neat and tidy.'

Mrs. Seth, the ophthalmologist's wife, Mrs. Borkar, the anesthetist's wife, Mrs. Khadilkar, the pediatrician's wife are just that – wives.

They are enjoying this whole exercise.

An untidy house, not managed properly by a working woman!

'No wonder…!' one of them mutters as if she has found an explanation for Dr. Patwardhan's death.

This is just the kind of glorious situation they seek to explain their lives.

Mother will have to explain this disorder.

Did the disorder happen last night?

Or, is the disorder a result of years of neglect?

Did the disorder happen last night?

Or did last night happen because of the neglect?

Mother should not have to explain anything to these women.

Mother is beautiful, intelligent, capable. Mother is better than all of them.

Mother has to be protected.

This is Mother's house. This is Baba's and Mamma's and Vinu's and Lalita's house.

It has to be kept hidden from these women.

Baba is dead. This is Mamma's and Vinu's and Lalita's house.

Lalita has to protect the house.

Protect the untidy corners from unkind eyes.

In this badly kept house, the women have not been able to even find a decent change of clothes for the little girl.

Trying to cover for mother, Lalita manages to literally push them out of her room.

She finds and wears a frock and seems to be searching for something.

She looks at the unwieldy ball made by various items of her underwear.

The child finds that some are too old, not fitting anymore, some waistbands have lost elasticity, some elastics tied into a knot in an attempt to tighten the sagging elastic maybe, a useless knot now for the elastic has snapped in an invisible place and many such panties are knotted up.

And none are wearable.

Lalita sees that the door of Mother's bedroom is locked.

Anuradha Auntie ushers Lalita out.

Lalita passively allows herself to be led.

Nobody has the time to realise that the little girl has not worn any underwear.

Only she knows .

She awkwardly holds on to her frock.

As she will hold on to her frock, then her skirt, and finally her saree.

She will be conscious of this fact.

When she is a woman, she will not allow herself to feel any desire for people can see right into her.

Dirty woman.

Exposed woman.

Vulnerable girl.

Does everybody know that she is not wearing panties?

Why are they looking at her?

They are looking at her to see how a ten-year-old looks at a Father's dead body.

It is apparent that the post-mortem examination is over. Two people are cleaning the table. The body has been transferred to a stretcher.

It is raining heavily. In the compound of the cottage hospital, there is a huge crowd.

Lalita watches from a distance. She is tense, but controlled, very dignified for her age.

Some male nurses wheel out Father's body on a stretcher. Various nurses, ayahs, ward boys and doctors come and touch Father's feet. A colleague, a teacher has been lost. They are wearing smart hospital uniforms.

In contrast, there is another group – priests half-dressed, noisy – they seem ugly to Lalita.

They take charge – literally claim the body from the hospital staff.

They take the dead body away for cremation. They cover it with garlands, performing rituals.

Lalita sees Father's stethoscope fall off. Her eyes are full of tears.

A little away Lalita sees some rural people, probably patients, crying and paying their respects. They are truly grieved. The crowd makes way.

Lalita clutches her frock as she goes to view her Father's body.

From that very crowd emerges Lalita, the thirty-four year old one.

***

Thiry-four because that is the age she is now.

But it could be any age.

For that is what you do when you don't care about a child — you make an uncared for woman.

That is what happens when a child is beaten up — an adult, battered all her life.

And every woman who is sweating at a job interview is ten years old again and is being told how bad she is at everything she does, how she will never be as good as that cousin.

Lalita has become a woman who will always feel watched by eyes she does not want.

Lalita will not want any eyes to see her, even the eyes of a man she may want.

She will not allow herself to want because of those unwanted eyes.

Unwanted eyes always on her.

That is what happens when someone looks at a child, when someone notices that a child has not been dressed to protect.

That the child is not protected by her mother.

This child will become a woman who will never enjoy a man's eyes on her because of the nausea that is accumulating at the base of her throat now.

For Bhatji is looking at her now.

Lalita, now thirty-four, kneels beside the body. Stiffly, she clutches her dress tightly.

A priest tells her to do namaskar.

She bends over, and puts her head on her father's feet.

Her bare legs are exposed.

When she sits up she realises that the priest is looking at her thigh. It is very awkward for her to adjust the frock.

She looks afraid, invaded.

Tucking the frock between her thighs, she reaches out to touch the sheet.

The sheet is tightly draped on Baba's body.

Her frock is loosely hanging around her body.

She has tucked the front of the frock between her thighs, leaving very less material at the back.

It flies up.

Are the parts touched by the cold breeze visible to everybody?

The humiliating breeze has travelled between her thighs and has entered a deep place.

Her consciousness.

And her unconsciousness; for she will have nightmares.

An insect crawls up her legs.

It lays eggs inside her.

Many tiny insects will crawl back down.

The insect will enter her when she is twelve, when she has just learned from friends' whispers that something is laid inside and a baby comes out. Something from a man's body.

Twelve is also the age when a man will look at her budding breasts and she will feel angry and frustrated.

Then, she will decide to not let it affect her.

To ignore the gaze.

Don't animals look at her? Does she let that affect her?

And insects.

So men are insects.

So there is the threat of an insect laying something inside her. And, how can a baby come out then? So insects will crawl down.

An insect will have crawled up.

The insect knows that she is not wearing panties.

Do all these people, the mourners know?

Will people always know?

Bhatji knows.

She will tell his name to Baba.

Baba will hit him.

One slap from Baba's hand will send Bhatji on his way to the temple yowling in pain.

Baba has strong hands.

***

Do strong hands become weak when they are dead hands?

For Baba is dead.

His hands are folded, confined under the sheet.

The child Lalita cries.

She wants to see her father's hands.

She tugs at them in vain.

Broad, strong, and beautiful — Baba's hands.

Partially submerged in water.

Glowing in the sunshine.

Dark, struggling, reaching out – Lalita's hands.

She will be safe if she can somehow hold those hands.

Father stands in shoulder deep water, Lalita swims towards him, she is a bit scared, Father encourages her, she reaches him and is scooped up in his arms. He then turns his cheek.

A fair cheek, a faint stubble because it is Sunday, he has not shaved.

She will press her cheek to his. They both know that and so he turns his cheek.

A blackened cheek, the stubble singed because he is dead.

***

Thirty-four year old Lalita bends down to kiss her dead Father's face. She stops suddenly when she sees the priest looking at her. She starts sobbing.

The priest looks at her thighs.

His enjoyment of her struggle to keep the frock down is unbearable.

The thirty-four year old woman still feels nauseated when she thinks of his face.

The ten-year-old child vomits.

The stretcher is lifted up; they were just waiting for this one last visitor – the daughter.

And now, look what she has done.

Baba is lifted up, Lalita watches, she can never touch his hands now.

One more paroxysm.

A splitting head.

She can never touch Baba's hands now.

She wants a hand to hold her forehead.

Just as she feels her head is going to give way, break-will the contents of her skull also spill like the vomit?

She can never touch Baba's hands.

A hand on her forhead.

Zaid's hands.

Zaid is Khala's son.

Khala must be around somewhere.

Khala would take Lalita home.

Khala will have a pair of panties for Lalita.

Khala was here, Lalita can close her eyes; then the other eyes will disappear.

But Khala has not been allowed to be here.

She will have to stare back at the unwanted gaze.

She will have to fight it on her own.

Lalita cannot close her eyes.

***

Her eyes are closed.

Zaid enters the library holding some books in his hand. He sees her, slows down and goes to where she is sitting.

He starts to put his hands over her shoulders but keeps them on the back of the chair instead. Lalita senses his presence. The two are still for a while. Lalita slowly relaxes. They continue to be quiet like this.

Their silences are comfortable with each other.

Their silences begin to hum quietly.

A strain of Raga *Megh Malhar*.

The raga is supposed to bring on rain. Now, the promise of rain brings on the raga.

There is always a promise of something when Zaid and Lalita are together.

But there is always the contrast between reality and the promise.

Zaid sees the tear.

'You need to stop feeling sad and try anger for a change.'

She holds an urn close to her chest.

'Angry? At whom?'

Zaid takes the urn and keeps it on the table.

'After her death, you are the head of the family, and should act like one.'

'Act like Ma?'

Zaid and Lalita laugh.

Various childhood incidents demand to be remembered as funny.

The incidents need not be painful any longer.

The incidents may be jokes shared by these two people.

The incidents demand a catharsis.

And so, Zaid and Lalita laugh.

Suddenly, Zaid becomes very serious.

'Sometimes, you do, you know.'

When Karim Uncle became serious like this, when he could see something in Baba that Baba did not want to talk about, Baba changed the topic.

'Do not take any favours from that right-wing party' and 'They are gaining importance here Doc; ugly religious divide will dirty our Konkan if we let them reign, if a man like you bows down to them.'

Sometimes Dr. Patwardhan was tired, if he had come to his friend's house to forget all the politics, to simply talk about their cricket team back at the Belgaum military school, sometimes Dr. Patwardhan was too tired.

He did not have the strength to think about the truths that his friend was pointing out.

It was okay then; the real problem would not have to be acknowledged.

Baba would just say, 'What's happening at court Karim?'

And Karim Uncle would talk about his work, knowing that he had made his point, knowing that Dr. Patwardhan would think about it later.

'What's happening at court, Karim?'

Lalita does not have to say even that much.

'Gastroenteritis has broken out in Mokhada. You know how it is,' says Dr. Zaid.

He talks about his work, knowing that Lalita is allowed to not listen. He does not want her to listen; he wants her to think about her future.

***

But Lalita is thinking about the past, another epidemic.

There is an epidemic and the cottage hospital is understaffed. Nurses and other members of the staff are working in makeshift arrangements. Lalita, who is fourteen years old and Zaid, eighteen years, are the youngest of the volunteers.

Zaid makes the oral rehydration solution. Lalita tries to feed it to a small baby. The baby cries. The mother holds his hands. Lalita is tired.

A whistle. The baby is distracted, and swallows the solution.

Zaid smiles. Lalita looks at him. Her fatigue disappears instantly.

A nurse comes up to them with a tray in her hands.

'All volunteers have to take the cholera injection.'

Zaid quickly rolls up his sleeve and takes the injection.

Lalita makes excuses.

'I'll have to ask Ma.'

The nurse has already refilled the glass syringe.

'She has, in fact, reminded me about this today. Come on, I have no time for all this.'

'Sister, can I give it?' asks Zaid, already picking up a moist cotton swab from the tray.

'But you are only in the first year. You people have had only cadaver dissection.' protests the nurse.

But the syringe is already in his hand. He pushes the piston, a tiny bit of fluid comes out of the needle. He does not even look at it.

He is looking at his frightened friend.

'You've only operated on cadavers.' says the nurse again.

'So what difference does it make? Look at her. She's half dead with fright anyway,' laughs Zaid and quickly administers the injection.

Zaid, at eighteen years and Lalita, at fourteen years look at each other and smile.

Lalita at thirty-four and Zaid at thirty-eight look at each other and smile.

So much promise — of work, of purpose.

Of life.

Life had made them a promise.

They had broken the promise life had made.

Sometimes by bringing together two people who are right for each other, life makes a promise.

The two people are meant to honour this promise.

And if they haven't been able to fulfil it, this is all they can do.

Smile wryly.

Look at each other with love and despair.

Lalita and Zaid look at each other and smile.

They stand midway between his car and the house. Tall trees surround them. There are dark clouds in the sky.

Lalita is about to break down.

Zaid holds her head with both his hands.

'The women remember your sessions on reproductive health and that corny song...' He invites her to his place of work, his home.

'I will come...,' she accepts his invitation.

It is the least she can do.

***

Zaid gets into the car.

He thinks about what she has rejected, but it would be unfair to burden her with it now.

And anyways, how can there be acceptance or rejection between them?

They are parts of each other.

'I will come,' she says again.

'Preferably without those boring social worker type charts?' teases he.

Lalita looks at him.

She does not want him to go.

She snaps at him. 'Must I laugh just to appreciate the effort?'

Zaid looks at her with affection.

'Just because I told you to try anger, it does not mean you have to try it on me.'

Now, Lalita really smiles.

Her hand on the rolled down window.

His hand reaches out to hers, but does not touch hers. It rests on the window, next to her hand.

He drives away. She looks at his car in the distance.

The harsh sunlight shines directly on Lalita's face. She starts walking back towards the house.

***

She sees Vinodini talk to a group of people. Mahesh sits close by. He looks away when Lalita looks at him. He has been looking at Lalita and Zaid. Lalita catches his eye and looks at him for a while.

He is surprised by a new confidence which Lalita seems to have acquired.

Vinodini seems to have acquired the persona that

Mother used to reserve for the press. Lalita looks at her sister as she talks to three reporters from the local press.

Vinodini speaks in a flat monotone.

Mechanically, as if she has been 'programmed'.

'...to manage the property, do social work and look after the home.'

Lalita flinches at 'social work'.

Vinodini knows she would; that is why she has used the term on seeing her sister approach.

Nalini knew Lalita would flinch at the word 'servant'.

Nalini used that term for Umabai, for Shanti, for Mali – Lalita's friends.

And now Vinodini too has learnt how to make Lalita flinch.

And more.

'...especially, after our father deserted us,' she tells the reporters now.

Lalita walks away from them.

At the back of the house is a dark room. Water is heated there.

She passes the clump of banana plants that feed on the dishwater.

She smiles at the memory of the rhythmic movement of Umabai's buttocks as she washed the vessels, squatting, her knees exposed.

Lalita enters the kitchen through the back door.

She needs comfort, warmth.

There is so much to be done.

She has to write that stupid essay.

She needs a drink.

Does the cupboard still hide the bottle of rum in a brown paper packet?

Baba is drinking from that bottle.

'I want you to remember that I love all of you very much,' says Baba as he hugs the ten-year old.

'You have to help me with that essay.'

'I have made a mistake and made your mother very angry.'

'That sounds exactly like me. She will forgive you Baba.'

Just as she is kissing him good night, his cigarette burns her hand.

'Just while going, I hurt my child.'

He kisses her hand again and again.

Vinu cries out aloud, she is cranky tonight, Mother is trying to put her to bed.

As if to include Vinu, Baba repeats, 'I love all of you very much.'

Lalita puts her cheek against his.

She looks out of the window.

She can see Vinodini talking to people in the garden.

'Father did not desert us Vinodini. He died. Alone, on the road — in the middle of the night, he burnt himself to death,' screams Lalita.

Vinodini of course, cannot hear.

Oh for a drink.

For at least the smell of rum.

***

'You stink of rum, you coward.'

It is for his own good that Mamma has to tell Baba not to drink; Lalita hides behind the door.

'I don't want to hide; I don't want to be a coward anymore, Nalini,' says Baba.

Mother looks displeased, as usual he tries to make her laugh.

'You'll have that big press conference you always wanted Nalu; now that they are giving us television to watch the Asiad games, maybe you'll be on TV too!'

She does not laugh. Lalita has a picture of Appu, the mascot of the Asiad games. This Appu...

But wait, Baba is telling Mamma something.

'I will tell everything. I will expose Naik who gave me money to contest the elections as an independent candidate, just to divide my party's traditional voters.'

'And what does that make you, Indrajeet?' interrupts Mamma, 'And what do you mean "my" party? The party that did not give you a ticket?'

She laughs pointing all the fingers of her palm at him.

'That's one thing Naik's party and your party have in common — they both knew you were incapable of winning an election.' He looks at her fingers as they become stiff and come close to his face.

He holds that accusing hand.

'Let's throw the money back on their face, Nalini. Let me confess to our people. I will tell my people that I made a mistake. Then, it's up to them...'

'Your people?' she pulls her hand out of his pleading grasp.

'Yes, my people, Nalini; they have known me since I was a child, they have known us from before I was even born.'

'And what will your people have to say when they read this?'

She holds a letter in her hand.

He holds out his open palms in front of her.

It is not just the letter he is asking for.

Dr. Indrajeet Patwardhan is asking for his wife.

'Help me', says he.

'Help you? Why? How has your affair helped me? Has it improved my self-respect? Has it helped to account for all these years in this dump?'

She puts the letter in the safe.

Her faces the open cupboard when she makes her final threat,

'If you open your mouth, Indrajeet, I too will call a press conference of my own.'

Baba looks at her in shocked appeal.

'And what money are you going to throw at Naik's face? It is gone already. I have made the down payment on that bungalow in Pune.'

Baba looks defeated. Threats from loved ones can be borne as momentary expressions of anger. But to know that a loved one has betrayed one's trust is difficult to bear.

Yet, he too has betrayed her trust.

He walks out of the main door.

Lalita runs to the window.

Father is so drunk, should he be allowed to drive?

He turns on the ignition.

Mother holds the door open.

Maybe Mother will stop him from driving.

Is Mother telling him something for his own good?

Instead, Lalita hears,

'Now that you have deserted your family in the worst possible way... '

Father holds her hands.

'Nalini, Nalini, what deserted?'

Mother pushes away his hands.

'Why don't you really go away?'

Lalita calls out from the window. But no sound comes out.

Mother bangs the door shut.

'Or better still — why don't you just DIE?'

Father drives away.

***

The family drives to a temple. The family — Lalita, eleven years old, Vinodini now three and Mother are still a family even though Baba has driven away. They have not become another family just because Baba is dead.

The priest says, of course, he knows their name, as Mother gives him a coconut and a bunch of bananas. Lalita can hear 'Patwardhan' punctuating the sing-song that the priest chants to the God.

This priest is not like the dhoti-clad half-naked Bhatji in the city.

He is not a brahmin, Mother has told her. He is not called Bhatji, he is a Gurav.

He is an ordinary man. He is a local. Lalita likes him. He is one of Baba's people. He is one of her people.

It has been a year since Lalita has been among the people. It has been a year since Baba died.

His god too is different from the orange city-gods.

A big black statue with beautiful silver eyes.

Black.

Dressed in a small white dhoti, and a sleeveless black jacket.

He has a Ghongdi – a rough hand-woven blanket- thrown on his shoulders.

This shepherd is one of her people.

Lalita misses her people.

She also is looking for a God.

Can this dark, big shepherd become her God?

The Gurav knows the story of his God.

'The god walks throughout the night – up the hills, in the jungles... Look here, his chappals are worn out.'

He picks up a pair from a big pile of old chappals kept in a tray. Next to it, in another tray are some new pairs given as offering.

The Gurav is proving his story by showing them the dusty, worn out underside of the chappal.

Lalita looks up at the statue.

A burning car.

A man enveloped in flames.

A burning man running helter skelter.

Did he change his mind about dying when he saw that his hands were on fire?

Did he scream for help?

'Where were you then?' screams Lalita at her new God.

If he walked the hills, why did he not save Baba?

Why did you not save him?

Screaming at the new God.

And Baba?

Why did he not think even for a moment about his daughters before killing himself?

Why did you die?

Screaming at Baba.

Why did you not think of me?

Why did you not care about me?

Why do you not take care of me?

Screaming at the shepherd, screaming at Baba.

Always.

A girl abandoned by her father is doomed to scream at every man.

To scream at the God.

She has a fierce look on her face. Mother naturally assumes that the anger is directed at her.

Mother does not know that her little girl is screaming at Father.

Has Mother known that the anger was directed towards Father, she would have remembered herself screaming at her own father.

Then Mother could have held the daughter close to her breast, and the child would be comforted.

Instead, Mother assumes that the child's anger is directed at her and so she gears up for a fight.

And because the abandoned child will scream forever, the conflict with Mother will be for ever.

So, the child will be entirely abandoned.

And Mother, tired of the conflict, will feel she is tired of the child.

Looking at Lalita's face, Nalini thinks she 'knows what's coming'.

'I know that expression. Itching for a fight with Mamma.' says she.

They are leaving the temple. Mother turns towards the god to make one final namaskar. Her eyes are closed. She mutters a prayer.

Lalita looks at another family. The father holds his child in his arms. The woman is bedecked with jewels. She wears flowers in her hair.

Mother, bereft of any jewellery, in a white saree. She has bent down to put on Vinodini's shoes.

Vinodini playfully tries to prevent it.

Lalita puts her arms around mother's neck.

'Let me do that.'

Lalita fastens the sandal buckles and holds her sister by her armpits as she jumps off the wall on which she was perched for Lalita to buckle her shoes.

Mother has taken the moment to lean against the wall.

Her hand reaches to the back of her neck.

It has been a year now since her mangalsutra was broken, Lalita wonders whether it still hurts her.

Or does she just miss the feel of her mangalsutra on her bare neck?

'I never want to fight with you Mamma.'

***

'I never understood why you fought with her.'

Mahesh looks straight ahead at the windscreen as he says this; he has been thinking about the relationship between his wife and mother-in-law.

Lalita and Vinodini are in the back seat of the car. To talk to anyone other than Lalita, Mahesh of course has to look at them, eye contact and all– just like the books prescribe; so he turns behinds and looks at Vinodini.

'You know, in our worst fights, when your sister refuses to react…'

'"Madam overreaction" herself refusing to react?'

Vinodini joins in; somebody has to acknowledge this attempt at bringing some humour into this sombre occasion. He notices it and they grin at each other.

Lalita hides her smile with her *dupatta* and pretends to cough. She will not be a part of this; as usual, the joke is on her.

And yet, she knows that Vinodini has joined in, perhaps even Mahesh has started this conversation because she, Lalita, looks sad.

They want to make her smile.

But the way they go about ridiculing her.

Yes, that's the way families are. The things that will make you most uncomfortable will be said.

The family observes little aspects of your behaviour that you yourself do not notice. Mahesh says to Vinodini,

'One sure way to provoke her, make her angry is to say something bad about your mother.'

Lalita looks out of the window.

Dust rises on the side of the Poona-Nasik highway. On the road itself, the tar gives out fumes because of the heat. A truck coming from the opposite side overtakes recklessly. For a moment it seems as if it is going to crash into this car. Then it swerves to the left.

Lalita closes her eyes. Her lips are pursed, her nose crinkled. Her fingers are on her forehead. She pushes her eyebrows together. She presses her eyes hard.

Merely closing her eyes is not enough to keep out some images.

A totally burnt car.

Only the discoloured, destroyed, metal frame remains.

Lalita opens her eyes.

'Petrol.'

Vinodini's hip accidentally touches Lalita's left hand that lies in the space between them as Vinodini takes a magazine from Mahesh, who sits in the front seat.

Neither has heard her.

So, she speaks a louder this time.

'I can smell petrol.'

But Mahesh and Vinodini do not pay heed. 'The others must have reached already,' Mahesh is saying to Vinodini.

She looks up to tell Mahesh again, and instead sees her own face.

A callused, dark hand adjusts the rear view mirror. Reflected in it is Lalita's tense, anxious face.

The driver's right hand puts on the left indicator.

***

The driver, Vilas Gavde is a rough looking, forty-five year-old man. He has a two-day-old stubble. He has tucked tobacco in the right corner of his mouth, under his lower lip.

It affects his speech noticeably.

'Let us find some shade,' says he as the car slows down and starts moving to the side.

'What happened?' Mahesh asks.

'If Madam smells petrol, we'd better check.'

The car pulls over to the side and stops under a tree. Vilas gets out of the car and opens the door for Lalita. She steps out. He unties a canvas water bottle from his cab. He nods to her. She bends down with her palms forming a cup to drink from. He pours the water. Lalita drinks and also splashes some on her face.

Vinodini has opened her laptop. Mahesh looks at his watch. They are least interested in Lalita. Everyone finds the heat unbearable.

The hood of the car engine is open. Lalita puts one hand on the car and peeps inside. Vilas is on the other side.

He looks up at her.

The driver comes over to her side.

The driver stands very close to her.

He lifts up his shirt.

Lalita is shocked.

She steps back.

For a brief moment, it seems as though he is going to make some rude gesture.

Lalita looks at his face. His eyes are filled with tears.

Now, she looks down at his body.

Running across his chest is a large ugly scar.

'Truck accident. Lung collapse. Your father did the operation.'

Lalita stretches out her hand.

Lalita ,ten years old, swims towards her father. The water reaches his shoulders. He smiles encouragingly.

Lalita ,thirty-two years old, swims upstream.

She can see only his hands in the distance.

Lalita wants to reach them.

She will be safe when she touches them.

Baba's hands, broad, strong, and beautiful.

Partially submerged in water. Glowing in the sunshine.

Lalita's hands, dark, struggling, reaching out...

Lalita places her hand on the scar. She closes her eyes.

Vinodini and Mahesh are far away, their view, even if they could be bothered to look at Lalita, is obstructed by the raised hood.

Vehicles whiz past.

Nobody notices this strange sight of a driver standing with his shirt bundled up and this woman touching his chest.

This beautiful sight when Lalita's restless face is peaceful.

Her right hand placed flat on the scar.

Her left hand, the fingers slightly bent, just touching her right hand as they slowly move along the length of the scar.

Lalita's hands finally touch Father's. She holds on to them. Her body relaxes. Hands and legs spread in the water. No longer struggling, the child dips her head into the water.

It starts drizzling.

Raindrops on Lalita's face, she opens her eyes.

Vilas' hand on the rear view mirror and reflected in it, Lalita's smile.

***

'I think the problem is solved Sir,' says the driver as he turns the ignition key.

Mahesh checks the time. Vinodini rolls up her window.

Vilas adjusts the mirror as the car starts again. The mirror shows the road.

Lalita's face emerges out of the window.

She takes in deep breaths.

She opens her mouth to catch the rain.

A little girl in a car, moving in the opposite direction does exactly the same thing.

Lalita waves to her.

The car travels over a bridge.

Trees line the banks of the river that flows under the bridge. Buffaloes cool off in the shallow parts.

The river flows away in search of a wilder, better place.

The river wants to meet the sea.

The river wants to be one with her God.

***

Instead, the river finds herself in the service of religion.

Her course is diverted to facilitate the cleansing of men.

The river is flanked by man-made structures.

Temples, platforms and steps.

Steps, so that anyone wanting to wash off his dirt can decide how deep he wants to go, can measure the depths he dares to enter.

There is no need to blindly jump into the river, face whatever might lie in the depths.

There is no risk of being crushed by rocks in the shallow part itself.

The distance he is prepared to travel can be measured.

The river has no such choice.

The river has to compulsorily take All the dirt, All the sins.

Ugly waste is generated when people throw the remnants of religious rituals like flowers and food into the water. Plastic bags have floated to the banks. The water is visibly polluted.

Powerful, oppressive priests order people around. Money is exchanged. Families perform various rituals on the 'ghats' along the river.

Anxious, believing, trusting faces.

***

Grieving faces.

Lalita and Vinodini are both lost in thought.

Mahesh and Shriram Bhatji are at the centre. Bhatji ties *darbha* grass around Mahesh's finger like a ring. Vinodini prays, her hands joined devoutly.

Lalita stares at the urn, which has now been opened. Grey ashes.

Ashes in another urn.

A small bone in the ashes. Lalita looks on. Her nose is red.

Shriram Bhatji is a little afraid of those nostrils that flare when she happens to look at him.

He talks to Vinodini instead.

'Vinu *beta* once the crow eats the food, we will know that her soul is free.'

Lalita looks at him.

His body.

The body that is Shriram Bhatji.

Shriram Bhatji wearing a dhoti, his legs crossed.

His hands scoop out *ghee* from a tin, mix rice, *ghee* and black sesame seeds together, knead the mixture and mould it into three balls. Place the balls, on the grass spread out on the ground. Place three betel nuts in a row. Point to each of these, one by one.

'Your grandfather, your father and this is your mother.'

He looks at Lalita's face and can see that she is angry.

She looks at the betel nut.

To reduce people to bodies.

To think of a person as flesh.

And then when that flesh is burnt, give its name to a betel nut.

A betel nut won't attack you for burning the flesh it once was.

A betel nut won't take revenge for the person it represents.

To reduce a human being to a harmless inanimate object.

To have a betel nut represent Mother.

Nalini, in her thirties, is smartly dressed in a crisply starched Calcutta handloom saree and a doctor's coat.

She has her hands around the hugely pregnant abdomen of a patient. Nalini sits at her huge desk and talks to a couple.

It is obvious that she inspires awe in them.

Nalini in the operation theatre.

Nalini holds a suction tube in her hand. A baby, just born, is lying still. Nalini' puts out her hand. A syringe is put into it.

A needle points at the baby's heart. The baby cries. Lalita's ten-year-old face looks through the circular glass in the door.

Nalini gestures Lalita to come in. She lets her hold the infant.

She looks proud of her work.

Dr. Nalini Patwardhan.

The betel nut.

Lalita looks helplessly at the incongruity of it all.

Shriram Bhatji repeatedly pours water from a copper vessel in his left hand over his right clenched palm and lets the water flow over the right thumb. Vinodini keeps looking at this.

Vinodini looks anxious.

Lalita sees that everybody is worried that the crow has not touched the food.

Shriram Bhatji and a local priest make caw-caw sounds. She covers her mouth with her saree to hide her laughter.

The sounds suddenly seem deafening to Lalita. She looks at Shriram Bhatji's face. There is something evil about the man.

Lalita gets up. She steps over some flowers, a bag,

and Attya's leg to make way for herself.

She walks away towards the river. Attya's cries are exaggerated.

'God knows what wish of hers has remained unfulfilled.'

If the crow does not eat, the soul has an unfulfilled wish.

Souls with unfulfilled wishes are dangerous.

***

Shriram Bhatji relocates the plantain leaf full of food. He pours some water on the ground and places the leaf there.

Is this done to cheat the crow?

To make it think this is a new offering?

Why will a crow be attracted to what it thinks is a new offering? Why had the crow rejected the old offering? When it tastes the food it will recognise the family. Will the crow discover that families always have exactly the same thing to offer?

The unwanted offering.

The exposed offering.

The *dal* on the rice has dried up. The *koshimbir* has given out water from the cucumber and curds used in it.

Lalita walks on. She stares straight at the river.

She shudders as Shriram Bhatji calls out to 'the soul of Nalini' in a loud voice.

'...the marriage of your younger daughter...'

'...your charities to the temple will continue.'

Lalita is disgusted.

She reaches the river.

***

Lalita climbs down the steps of the ghat. Lalita looks at a poor mother and her two-year-old son playing in the water. The woman is kissing her child's face repeatedly and noisily. The baby is delighted.

At a distance, an older boy watches.

He is about ten years old, very dark and thin. His head is totally shaved, except for a little tuft, a *shendi*.

Someone calls out to the woman.

Lalita looks around to see an older woman, probably the mother-in-law. She wants this young woman to join the rituals – they have not come here to play with children in the water.

Did her own mother-in-law do the same thing to her?

Women will realise their full potential only when they have a *complete* perception of their *shared* past.

Women.

Sisters.

Is that why she felt incomplete?

Did Vinodini feel incomplete too?

A shared past.

And a complete perception of it.

Meanwhile, the children's mother wrings out water from her loose hair.

Without even looking at her older child, she roughly gives the baby to him.

Lalita sits on the lowermost steps, very close to the water. The woman walks by Lalita on her way up to the temple.

Lalita watches as he looks after the baby, keeps it safe, happy. Elbows on her knees, her palms cupping her cheeks.

She gestures that he should not go further, deeper into the water.

He obeys and immediately comes closer to the bank, near where Lalita is. He plays, with his back to Lalita.

While teaching his brother to swim, the boy also teaches him a word.

'Are you going to call me *Dada* forever? Don't you want us to be friends when we grow up?'

'Say Nivurti.' He teaches his younger brother.

Lalita taps him on the shoulder.

'Not Nivurti. Nivrutti. N-i-v-r-u-t-t-i,' says she.

He turns back to look at her. Lalita looks past him, at the baby.

The baby catches hold of the older brother's *shendi* and pulls it hard.

Lalita, shocked, is not angry at the younger sibling.

How can the older boy allow this?

He is in charge, so she shouts a question at him.

'*Ae Bala,* don't you feel like hitting him back?'

And the boy — Nivrutti — the older brother looks at her directly and answers slowly,

'By giving my little brother pain, will mine become less?'

Lalita looks gratefully at the boy.

She looks at the river.

Her disappointment at seeing the river bound in religion has hope, for at a distance, the river takes a turn around a bend of a hill.

The river disappears.

May be despite all this,despite being treated as a dustbin for rituals, beliefs, faith, it does flow freely after all.

The river is not a dustbin.

The river carries the sins to the sea.

The river's journey to the sea is a lonely one; she will always be alone.

The river chooses to do this.

The choice:

Should Lalita reveal some bitter truths?

Or will she grant Vinodini the false memories of an idyllic childhood?

A childhood that Lalita herself could only dream of.

It would be easy to live knowing that Vinodini was with her.

'Go in peace, Mamma. I am going to protect my baby sister.'

The sounds of cawing from a distance. Lalita stares at the river.

A crow flies. The crow eats the food. One more crow comes and starts eating. The family starts walking away.

'Will everybody be ready by eight tomorrow?'

Mahesh is back in his element once again—arrangements, logistics.

Vinodini is walking back with Anuradha Auntie. She is the only one to turn back and look towards the river.

Lalita is alone on the steps. She looks serene.

The river flows strongly crossing various obstacles. Little streams flow into it.

Sewage pipes are also emptied into it.

It carries all the dirt and yet looks beautiful.

***

All the dirt, for there are all kinds.

Lalita tiptoes in.

A fully dressed Mahesh lies diagonally across the bed. He dozes off like that when he is tired. Usually, this is a big relief for Lalita who then goes out to sleep on the couch.

But today, he wakes up.

Mahesh looks at Lalita.

There are all kinds of beautiful.

She seems strong now, and beautiful.

'Vinu said you'd want to be alone. Let's order some food for you,' says her husband.

'Go back to sleep. Did you take your tablet?'

None of his patients or friends would guess that Dr. Gune has been diagnosed as diabetic for the last two years.

She has neglected his diet for the last few days, Lalita feels. It is time to go home and start cooking those measured meals.

Time to go home and a reason to stay home.

'I was waiting for you to come, so I could change into my pajamas.'

He sounds like a little boy. Lalita gets his clothes from their bag.

Mahesh sees how even on such a trip, she has not forgotten to carry his towels. He does not like to use any other.

He wraps the towel around his waist and begins taking off his trousers — clothes changing habits from a small house with four siblings.

There were other habits, to do with food and other personal aspects of his life, that none of those people who admired Dr. Mahesh Gune had any idea of.

Lalita had looked upon all those habits with affection, with love.

And what had he done?

One day, a towel wrapped around his waist, he had stood in front of her. It was in the middle of the night; they'd been having a fight. Thinking that he had stood there to make up, she had put her arms around him, and he had slapped her.

There had been other such occasions.

'I gave you so many scars,' says he.

Lalita puts a framed photograph of Aphra into the bag, after looking at it for a moment.

'Not only scars,' says she; her daughter has after all come from t his marriage.

Lalita goes into the bathroom and comes out wearing a nightgown. If she takes her time to have a bath, her husband will deduce that she is not listening to him.

Why is Mahesh saying all this tonight?

Why is he so different? What has come over him, she wonders.

His changed manner has nothing to do with Mahesh, she realises, as he respectfully turns away to tug the towel off the pajamas that he has just pulled on.

A husband's manner towards his wife changes not because he has undergone a transformation, but because she has changed, because she acquires strength, because he sees her in a different light.

'When we got engaged, my friends at Karad said I was too *ghati* for you. They were right,' says he.

Lalita takes off her earrings.

'You looked so distant, so unattainable, Lalita, I subjugated you in the only way…'

The window slams shut and opens again. Lalita goes to shut it. She looks out.

She does not look at his face as he says,

'You tried to make me understand. It must have been difficult to tell me all those things.'

Lalita shuts the window.

But only the one who knows is the one who can hurt.

She switches off the light. She lies down next to him.

'Are you okay?'

'Very tired,' says she and realises how this is exactly the thing she says when he comes to her at night.

How did he feel about that? Did he come to her out of love, at least some of the time? Was it his way of trying to come close to her? Had she rejected his love?

But then there were those dirty pictures, those stories.

But then, even before all that started, Lalita, had felt nauseated by sex. Had she made her revulsion very obvious?

As if he knows what she is thinking about, he puts his arm around her,

'You clearly did not want me. So, I decided to imagine you were someone else...'

And she has craved to want, craved to want for herself, Lalita wants to tell him, but he's still talking.

'All that excessive cleaning after – just running to the bathroom – many a time, I wanted to hold you, apologise, but you were gone.'

'And then after I had heard those sounds from the bathroom – sounds of the harsh scourging off me, I no longer wanted to apologise. Being cruel to you seemed okay in return for the disgust you felt for me.'

Lalita wants to tell him that this 'harsh' cleaning was a habit she had formed long before she met him.

'You took a long time at it.' He's saying, '... you hoped I would get fed up of waiting and fall asleep.'

But how can she tell him that however long she took, she never felt clean, because it was her mind that had been dirtied.

Mahesh falls asleep after a while. She pulls a blanket over him.

She pulls their blanket over him.

Her husband.

The two times that he had betrayed her, she had been hurt.

Was she so possessive about him that even pornography caused such indignation?

Had Mother been hurt like this?

Yes, she had been hurt because her husband had first admired and then loved that environmental activist woman.

Yes, Mother had been betrayed, hurt, Lalita realised.

But was Baba's offence grave enough for the death penalty? Had Mamma sentenced Baba to death?

Had he killed himself to repent?

Had she, had he, why had they…?

Lalita cannot sleep.

Maybe a hot shower will help.

***

Moths cover the bathroom wall.

Moths are ghosts.

Moths are souls on parole.

Moths are on parole from a death walk.

A parole death walk on the bathroom wall.

Freedom — life for a day.

And bound by honour to end that day with death.

Moths bound by honour to fling themselves into a flame.

He had wanted a parole out of his life sentence.

A night of wings.

A night of wings to end in a flame.

What honour had it been that he had died to protect?

To think that she was part of her father's honour.

To know that the blame she put on him was unfair.

That he had not thought of his daughter once, before killing himself, before abandoning her.

It was his daughters that he had thought of, the shame that he would bring on them.

If Mother really exposed him in the way she threatened to.

The shame that he would bring to them if he lived.

And so he had chosen to die.

But Baba, I would have rather had you with us, alive.

We could have faced anything if you were alive.

Don't die, Baba.

Don't burn yourself, Baba.

Don't fling yourself into a flame, moth.

Moths are troubled souls on a death-row parole.

***

Lalita has trouble falling sleep.

She can hear the purring of a cat.

Purring is a pleasant sound; well, at least to people who like cats.

This was the ugly meowing, the scary growling, the — well, the only effective way to stop it, she had learned, was to throw cold water out of the window.

She had learned to do that – throw water in the direction that the sound was coming from – and hope that some off it would touch the animal.

Once a cat had looked back at her, so actually looking at that furry animal was out of the question.

Its tail would be expanded and erect if it was making those sounds.

Its body would be stretched into an attacking pose.

The cat's eyes.

And the fur.

The fur.

She wants to scream.

Actually looking at the cats was definitely out of the question.

***

In the lounge, Lalita sees Vinodini sitting alone with a cup of coffee. A group of young people try to get rooms for the night. Lalita sees Vinodini look at them.

'You saw to it that I did not go for that Rajasthan class trip...,' says Vinodini.

'I'm sorry. I used to feel a little protective about you.'

Vinodini does not shift to make space for Lalita on the sofa.

'Little? When we walked out of a movie theatre, you would keep your hand in front of my chest. Barely bigger than me, you insisted on teaching me swimming yourself. No coach you said.'

Lalita starts walking back.

'But I never prevented you from being friends with the boys in your class, Vinu.'

She starts to climb the staircase. Vinodini stands at the foot of the staircase.

'What was your problem? That I was the better looking sister? You were jealous that unlike you, I had breasts?'

She raises her voice; this conversation is not over, so what if her sister looks tired; especially now that her sister is tired, for then, she, Vinodini, can win.

'By the time you had finished your brainwashing, by the time I went to hostel, I was completely paranoid.'

'So is that what you call it? Paranoia?' shouts Lalita.

She is angry that it is only when she is tired, when she is weak,and they know it that the people she either loved or trusted, choose to hurt her.

'Is paranoia the name you give to sluttish behaviour? Is paranoia the name for how you made sure I knew about your no-morals disgusting way of life, just so that I would be sad?'

'Yes, I slept around, but I never fell in love you know, Akku. I would have, if I had met someone alone, so to speak; but you were always there – warning me, worrying about me. I couldn't care. After a while, I just wanted more and more of the sex that you found so abhorrent. I have always been called a "loose woman"...'

'And my husband called me frigid.'

Lalita comes and sits next to her.

'It was not only you that I wanted to cover, Vinu, the walls I made around me were even thicker.'

Lalita touches her shoulder and Vinodini starts sobbing.

'No father to call me his pretty girl. And you literally hiding me away. I felt ugly. I am the frigid one Akku. I never liked any of it you know. Never felt anything.'

Lalita tries to put her arm around her sister. Vinodini pushes her hand away.

'I never felt anything. That is why I offered to give head,' laughs she, 'so the man wouldn't know how dry I was, how I didn't want him at all.'

Lalita cannot take this, she begins to get up.

'No. Stay. Listen.' She presses Lalita's shoulder down.

'You know how oral sex smells? The actual Thing of course has a mint or even banana flavoured condom on it...' laughs she.

'Yes, there is a banana flavour too,' her laugh is louder now.

'But the parts around it make me want to vomit – the hairy, sweaty parts smell of the man, of men, different men – none of whom actually stay the night, you know, Mrs. Gune.'

'Mrs. Gune.' She repeats.

She pinches Lalita's mouth between her thumb and a bent forefinger.

'Akku, meet your baby sister. Miss Vinodini Patwardhan — the blowjob specialist.'

'Taste the smells, dear sister,' says Vinodini as she kisses Lalita hard on the mouth.

***

The taste of blood.

Her tongue tries to determine whether Vinodini has bitten her or have her lips pressed against her own teeth and hurt themselves.

Lalita has walked some distance. She looks up at her room. Mr. and Mrs. Gune's room.

Mrs. Gune.

Did Miss Patwardhan know that she never really became Mrs. Gune totally because she always thought that her sister was not married, did not have a man of her own?

But the violence? Was that why she was lonely in the marriage, or did the violence come about because of her alienation from the marriage?

Mahesh had never talked like he has just a while ago. Mother's death, her going away allowed them to be themselves.

Mahesh talked for the first time. Had Mother's presence affected his relationship with her daughter?

But all that was unimportant, compared to what Vinodini has said tonight.

Her Vinu. Her baby.

What had Lalita done to her?

And she had been thinking of doing worse. She had wanted to burden Vinodini with her hurt. She had thought that would explain why she was always in conflict with Mother.

Vinodini will forgive me, she had thought; my sister will love me.

It does not matter now whether her sister loved her or not. Did Lalita love her sister? Would she love her unconditionally? That has been brought to test.

She had been thinking of burdening her sister.

Mother had stopped her.

I will not burden her with My truth, Lalita had promised, and the crow had eaten.

Every human being should be allowed to live with their own truth.

No human being should want to burden another with her own version of truth.

***

These revelations of versions of truth were worse than lies.

Especially when they were made in the name of love.

Lalita had always loved Vinodini.

And instead of crying over the imagined unrequitedness of that love, it was her responsibility to care for her sister now.

To give unanalysed, love.

For it did manage to reach love too, this habit of analysing everything that life offered.

Lalita reprimands herself for having felt superior to others even in her chronic self-pity.

She, Lalita looked carefully at something that others were too busy to look at.

Why were they busy?

They were busy with living the present moment.

Lalita had missed out on that.

Life.

The present moment – a combination of joy and sorrow; a mixture of truth and lies.

She had not enjoyed the present moment.

She had not lived.

She had been occupied with seeing the truth.

And Lalita had prided herself on being able to always see the truth. What use was this ability? What was so great about it?

Male authors... the thought of Zaid, his remembering that 'only women authors rule'... Male Authors have always made such a big deal of the search for truth. What was this Truth?

True, Lalita smiles to herself, true that truth was difficult to find, but what did you do once you found it?

For once you find it, you cannot ignore it.

And then, this truth that has found you refuses to leave.

The truth about Baba's death had found Lalita, had chosen her.

The knowing of it, could not bring Baba back; this truth was useless.

The useless truth became her burden.

To want to share this burden with her sister all her life, and tonight decide not to.

To want, instead, to just put the burden down.

To unwrap the weighted bundle that she has been carrying on her head, and to realise that it has been empty all along.

To realise that emptiness has weighed her down.

And now that she knows that emptiness has done this, she wants to destroy the emptiness, to fill it up.

***

The howling of the cats has not stopped. Lalita can see the leaves of a bush move as though the cats are inside. She sits on a bench and pulls her knees close to herself.

Precariously perched on a table, Lalita peeps under the table. She can see a cat.

She has a ruler in her hand.

If it tries to come out, she pushes it back in, scaring it with the ruler.

She is terrified.

Vinodini finds Lalita, she has been looking for her sister, may be she has been too harsh.

Yes, she has been harsh, for Lalita looks terrified. She sits on a bench, her knees pulled close to her.

Her knees pulled close to her, Akku is precariously perched on a table. She has a ruler in her hand. If it tries to come out, she pushes it back in, scaring it with the ruler. This is crazy behaviour, Mamma says; it has to be ignored, how will Akku become a brave girl otherwise?

Vinodini can see the leaves of a bush move as though the cats are inside. She throws a stone into the bush. Two cats run away. Lalita accuses Vinodini almost childishly.

'Why did you have to keep pet cats?'

'Mamma said it would help you overcome the fear.'

'Akka, instead of keeping the cat under your table, why didn't you muster just a little courage and throw it OUT? Throw that ruler at it?'

'It was your pet Vinu.'

***

Vinu's pet, and yet that day she had been scared to go close to it.

Her pet, Goldie.

One of her pets, there were many cats in the house.

Also in the house, was a scared girl, getting startled often.

Peering under beds before she entered a room.

Afraid that a cat might jump on her from the top kitchen shelf.

Closing both her ears with her hands to shut out the

meowing at night.

Getting up in the night to make sure a cat was not lying at the foot of her bed as it sometimes did.

Keeping a stick with her in bed.

Tapping the stick in front of her if she had to go to the bathroom at night.

Like a blind person.

Or an extremely frightened one.

Lalita, her sister.

Afraid of a pet.

And yet, that day when everyone was scared to go near Goldie, it was Lalita who went close and gave the cat a bowl of milk.

Goldie was Vinu's biggest female cat. This was going to be her third litter. Goldie was wild with pain. She had not eaten anything for twenty hours now.

The cat refused to come out of the cupboard. It sounded too scary for Vinodini to try to feed it.

Umabai kept a bowl of milk on the floor; she too did not open the cupboard and keep the bowl inside. If it kept wailing like that, and did not eat, Umabai told Vinodini, the cat would surely die.

How many deaths would that be? Vinodini thought. She sat on the last step of a staircase, opposite the cupboard. Not exactly opposite the cupboard, not too close.

How many deaths would that be?

How many cats would die if Goldie died?

How many kittens lay inside the cat?

Three?

So would four cats die then?

There would be thirty-six deaths then – nine times four?

Nine lives for each cat.

Thirty-six deaths if Goldie died.

But Goldie did not die.

For Akka came, took one look at her trembling Vinu and walked calmly to the cupboard.

She did not try to put the bowl inside. Instead, she opened the cupboard, just a little so as to not startle the cat.

Akka, so scared of cats, took care not to scare this one.

Then, gently, she brought Goldie out.

Holding the cat close to her chest, she rocked it.

Vinodini knew how that rocking felt; she knew how it was to be held close to Akka's chest.

The thiry-six cat-deaths would not happen now.

She looked at her sister's hand stroking the cat's back.

Goldie's tail slowly relaxed, and she stopped wailing.

The tail became thinner to reveal a paw sticking out from under the tail.

Vinodini was shocked and moved a step up the staircase. Lalita touched the paw and Goldie let out an angry meow and jumped out of the kind arms.

She went to the cupboard but did not climb in. Vinodini looked at the scratch on her sister's forearm as Lalita sat down beside the cat. This time, Goldie allowed her to touch the paw.

Why was Akka pushing back the paw?

Was she pushing back the kitten because surely, less kittens in the house was what she wanted?

Akka pushed the paw deep inside Goldie's body.

Vinodini decided to run away.

Now she was not scared only of Goldie; Akka looked fierce too.

Fierce and kind at the same time.

Like that strange woman – Nakusa.

Akka and Goldie seemed to have become partners in something that Vinodini could not understand.

So, she had chosen to run to her room.

She would ask Akka about it later.

But later, when she came back to the back verandah, Akka wasn't around.

Inside the cupboard, an old cloth was placed on a pile of *raddi*, newspaper. On the cloth was Goldie, fast asleep. The three new kittens made her forget everything.

She would soon forget the paw sticking out. She would forget to ask her sister what she had done to help the cat.

Today, she remembers that she had forgotten to ask one more thing.

How had Lalita got the courage to handle a wild Goldie?

Why had her ailurophobe sister helped a cat?

And today, twenty years later, Lalita had said, 'It was your pet, Vinu.'

***

Vinodini hopes Lalita has slept. She wishes that her sister will get some rest tonight.

'You will need to rest sometimes.' Nikhil had said while giving her the bottle of vodka. Did he think she would want to get drunk at a time like that, she had asked him. And he had said,

'You will need to rest sometimes.'

We all needed to rest sometimes.

She hopes Lalita is getting some rest. Hasn't she thought that just a while ago? Said it aloud in fact.

Is she drunk?

Is she sleepy?

It feels pleasant – this getting drunk all by herself in an impersonal room.

Of course, she has been drunk in impersonal anonymous hotel rooms before, but there has always been some act to put on.

For the first time, she is drinking alone and being herself.

It feels pleasant – this, being herself, drunk in a personal room.

Personal – only her own; so she can do personal things.

Even scratching as you like is such a pleasure.

Scratching is also scary.

There is a scratching sound outside the window.

And the sound of cats.

She should have asked Lalita to sleep in her room. But then they had parted so terribly.

She should have asked Lalita to sleep in this room. No, it is not because of the yowling of the cats that scares Lalita.

It is because Vinodini feels afraid sometimes.

Sometimes we all get afraid.

Sometimes when she is alone, sometimes when her sleep is restless, she wants her Akka to be with her.

Her sleep is restless when she drinks herself to sleep. She looks at the bottle, has she really drunk half the bottle?

Vinodini puts on her glasses, takes them off.

When faced with a disturbing sight, she takes off her glasses.

She has learnt this trick in her childhood.

'I was not scared,' she has often told her friends after a horror movie.

She has simply taken off her glasses in the scariest bits.

So when the others scream in terror she has defocused her way out.

She has learnt to defocus her way out.

Defocus her eyes and look bravely.

Defocused, distorted.

The object becomes distorted, therefore scarier. But it is easier to bear because of the remoteness it achieves.

Remote, unreal, distorted.

Like a dream, one could say; oh, she is sleepy.

But in a dream this trick of hers does not work.

She has had a nightmare since childhood. The chain of events is the same. The events occur.

So, to distance herself, she wants to defocus out the people.

After all, it works in her waking life.

Dreams do not obey the day time rules.

A thumb moves up and down a thread.

The dream senses her need to distance herself and just makes everybody more familiar.

The sounds of fighting tomcats.

Vinodini's body is drenched in sweat.

In the nightmare, she is not allowed to defocus what she does not want to see.

Nightmares bring seemingly unimportant actions into sharp concentrated focus.

A thumb runs up and down a sacred thread.

Scenes of emphasised innocuousness appear in nightmares.

So then, why are nightmares so frightening?

Nightmares choose trivial, innocuous scenes, and then blatantly exhibit the threat that was hidden in the day.

A thumb runs up and down the sacred thread across a hairless, obese torso.

The body clad in a dhoti moves closer.

A little girl's back-long silky hair reaching the hips.

Barefoot, she walks on.

Just as the man's hand is about to reach her hair, another girl's hand pulls her.

The other girl stands between her and the man.

The older girl's back – an unruly mop of curly hair.

***

Lalita's curly hair flies wildly all over her back.

She stands at the entrance of a temple.

Unruly, curly hair.

Lalita secures it with a rubber band.

She climbs over a high threshold.

Vinodini looks at the way her sister drags her foot along the stone surface of the step. Lalita will not gather up her saree and quickly step over the threshold.

Glad that she herself is dressed in her track suit, Vinodini starts walking towards the temple.

Vinodini peeps into the temple. She steps back and looks down.

Chappals, shoes and umbrellas are put in a pile. Lalita's pair of kolhapuri chappals. Vinodini sits down and begins to untie her shoe laces.

A pair of sports shoes next to kolhapuri chappals among the other footwear.

A little girl's dark feet, toes curled, the great toe, pressing on the next one.

Lalita stares at the feet and starts picking at the cuticle of her own great toe.

Vinodini's eyes are not accustomed to the darkness. They look around.

They meet Lalita's eyes but are not acknowledged.

She follows Lalita's gaze.

A little girl's dark feet, toes curled, the great toe, pressing on the next one.

Lalita and Vinodini stare at the child who is being put through some kind of ritual.

A wet frock clings to the child. She has bundled it and tucked it between her legs. She is repeatedly asked to stand up and sit down.

Vinodini sits down beside her sister. Lalita continues to look at the child. The child pulls the wet dress away from her chest. Her fingers pinch the cloth. The priest gives her a flower and some rice grains to hold in that hand.

For a moment, the child's eyes meet Vinodini's.

***

Her eyes are smarting.

Salt water hurts eyes.

And tears.

Lalita, sixteen years old, walks out of the sea, her clothes clinging to her. Religious rituals are being performed all around.

'Do we really have to walk all the way to the house in wet clothes?' she asks Mother.

But gets an answer from Shriram Bhatji.

'No no,' he smiles. 'You are supposed to bathe here and then go into the temple in wet clothes.'

Mother starts walking away from the sea, holding Vinodini by the hand.

Bhatji falls behind and walks with Lalita.

She is clearly uncomfortable.

They walk barefoot to the temple. It is a small lane, lined with small shops. Religious songs set to new filmi tunes blare from loudspeakers.

Shops selling sweets, pendants and other souvenirs. The under-employed, relaxed, shopkeepers chew tobacco, and comment on the devotees walking towards the temple.

They reach the temple.

Bhatji touches Lalita's shoulder as they climb the steps.

'Mamma.'

'The children will be hungry. Are we going to your home for lunch?' asks Mother to Bhatji

'I'm not hungry, Mamma. I want to talk to you.'

She looks at Bhatji and his assistant. She wants to talk to Mother alone. Mother buys a basket of flowers and coconut from a vendor on the steps. She hands the basket to Lalita.

She indicates that Lalita should come inside with her.

The basket is handed to the priest inside. Mother joins her hands. The priest starts the prayer.

Everybody joins their hands in prayer.

Where is the hand that joins her?

Lalita looks behind, where is Vinodini?

Shriram Bhatji gives Vinodini a pair of bright plastic bangles.

The child takes them and tries to put them on. The priest breaks the coconut. He chants mantras.

Shriram Bhatji takes the bangles from Vinodini's hands.

He presses her hand and forces them on her wrists.

Lalita sees how he squeezes her hand repeatedly, to push the bangles on.

'Vinodini.' She calls out to her little sister.

Bhatji is startled.

He deliberately presses the bangle.

The brittle plastic breaks.

There is blood on Vinodini's hand.

With a great show of caring, Bhatji snaps the bangle into two and throws it away.

Mother hits Lalita on the back of her head.

'Now look what you have done.' Mother hits her on her head again.

Vinodini looks at Lalita accusingly.

As if suddenly realising that Lalita is at fault.

Lalita is saddened by this confusion that has formed in her Vinu's mind.

She is worried about the piece of plastic which is still stuck in Vinodini's hand.

Between the base of her thumb and the wrist, the mark will remain and the little nutcase will check it to determine which of her hands is the right one.

'This is my right hand. The hand with the mark. Akku broke a bangle.' She will recollect.

Vinodini is already looking at her accusingly, for it is Lalita's fault that is being stressed upon.

'She behaves as if she is possessed by an evil spirit sometimes. Please do something Bhatji.' says Mother.

***

Vinodini looks at the scar on her hand.

The Akku-scar she had called it as a kid.

The Akku-scar it will be, always.

A sign of how her sister had wanted to protect her.

There had been blood.

There is blood on Akku's saree.

She has tucked it under her foot to cover the wound caused by a tear in the cuticle of her great toe.

The family that's performing the ritual on the child is getting rewarded for it.

Prasad is being served on plantain leaves.

Everybody sits in a row and eats from plantain leaves. Lalita gets up. Bhatji also gets up. Lalita goes to the courtyard where a big vessel of water is kept. Bhatji comes and gets out a mug of water and begins to pour it on her hands.

Lalita bends to wash her hands.

She sees that the man has been staring at her cleavage. She stands up and straightens her kurta.She looks at Mother. Mother is serving something to Vinodini.

Lalita looks away, walks away.

Lalita walks into the inner room where their luggage is kept. Mother and daughters are going to live in this room while in Gokarna. There are no hotels in this town, or rather, only-women families can't check into a hotel in a pilgrimage town. The priests rent out their houses to pilgrims.

The priests who tell you what rituals you need to conduct, what abhisheks you need to do.

An abhishek is the pouring of milk over the God.

Milk which could be drunk by children that God created.

Different quantities of milk depending on how rich the devotee is; how dreadful his sins.

To pour liquid over the God is to wash the devotee's sins away?

***

The room is lit only by an oil lamp near an ugly 'religious' painting. Lalita's hand tries to find the switch for the light. Bhatji's hand grabs it.

Lalita, the adult, the thirty-four-year-old that Vinodini knows, is afraid.

Vinodini knows how scared Lalita is.

The eight-year-old Vinodini stands at the door and sees her sister.

Bhatji pulls Lalita close to him. His left arm is across her chest.

The adult Lalita's chest.

Bhatji pulls the adult Lalita to him.

Even the recollection or fictional   narration of a child's breast being touched by an adult man is NOT to be allowed.

Earlier, on the beach, Bhatji had tried to kiss Vinodini on her cheek.

His thick lips had been about to touch her cheek when suddenly, her Akku had pulled her away.

'Your Mother is wrong. It is not that some ghost has taken possession of your soul,' Says Bhatji 'You are an evil spirit yourself.' He presses his right arm across her lower abdomen.

The adult Lalita's abdomen.

For when a lecherous man touches a child's abdomen in this heinous way, she will always feel that touch.

Maybe a man who loves her will make her forget for a while.

She will forget when she carries a child inside her.

But there will be times when she feels dejected, times when she is a little depressed and then she will remember that touch.

Lalita frees herself.

Sixteen-year-old Lalita runs out of the room.

She holds the hand of her eight-year-old sister and takes Vinu with her.

But before that, just as Lalita reaches the door, Bhatji sees that Vinodini has been standing there all along.

Bhatji smiles.

The priest looks at her and plays with the sacred thread running across his chest.

***

A priest, in a red dhoti, with *kajal* in his eye touches the sacred thread across his torso as he watches.

Vinodini notices this.

A priest 'accidentally' brushes against the child's body as he does *drishta kaadhna*, driving away the 'evil eye' by rotating a coconut, then flowers, and finally, some burning coal very close to the child's face.

A lot of smoke emanates from this. The child calls out to her mother.

'Aai.'

'Mamma', Lalita had called out to her Mother.

Lalita is scared. She pants and tells Mother something. Vinodini cannot hear what she says.

Nalini slaps Lalita. She holds her hand tightly, hurting her.

'I know you have a dirty mind, you ugly girl. But to talk about Bhatji like that – BITCH.'

Vinodini watches, how can Mamma slap Akku after what Bhatji has done to her?

Does Lalita deserve that?

Has Lalita done something bad?

Mother knows best.

It is best not to say or do anything.

It is best to forget.

She had forgotten.

Who was reminding her now?

Did Mother want Vinodini to remember?

Had Mother wanted Vinodini to know?

When she was alive, Mother's shadow had always separated Lalita from her sister. Why had she now, after her death, chosen to be the light?

Mother is dead

They are alone.

Yes, Vinodini has wanted some time with her Akku.

She has wandered into this smoke-filled temple to find her sister.

And she has found her where she had left her all those years ago.

***

The smoke covers Vinodini's face. Tears stream down her face.

Lalita sits a little behind her, almost fading into the background.

She bends her neck backwards to touch her head to the wall.

Both her hands cover her mouth as if suppressing a scream.

Vinodini kneels in front of her and gently tries to relax those fingers.

Lalita presses her mouth even harder.

Her face breaks into a terrible expression.

Vinodini puts her arms around Lalita. Both cry loudly.

Lalita's arms slowly hold Vinu.

A silence has fallen over the temple. Away from the sisters, the little girl on the *paat,* looks at them.

***

Mahesh and Shriram Bhatji are talking to each other. Lalita and Vinodini walk towards them, together.

'Okay Maheshrao, I will be seeing you soon I hope. Otherwise, you city people – you may turn up directly for the *varsha shradhh.*'

'Let's see...' replies Mahesh. 'Vinodini has to decide whether to sell... we will probably meet then.'

Vinodini totally ignores Bhatji. She looks past him at Mahesh.

'The house is a family matter Mahesh Bhaiyya.'

Shriram Bhatji tries to talk to her. When she does not respond, he goes and stands close to Lalita. He turns to Mahesh.

'I'll let Vinodini know what needs to be done.' he says.

Vinodini looks at her sister and tells Bhatji, 'Akka is the head of our family now. She will decide what is to be done.'

Lalita turns around to face Bhatji. Vinodini passes her bag to Mahesh.

So, she is also facing Bhatji.

Her tone is even sterner now.

'I don't think we will have a *shraddh.* In fact, Bhatji, you need not come to our home any longer.'

Shriram Bhatji looks at Lalita.

She is strong, unafraid.

***

The house is the same. However, it seems to look

brighter. The curtains are drawn apart, there is more light and colour in the rooms.

It is a hot summer morning. The ground is parched. The trees look dry.

Notes of Raga *Basant* on the Sarangi.

Lalita and her daughter look at a rainwater harvesting lake.

Vinodini has been shooting a documentary. A group of people, not part of the film team have been telling people about water.

Lalita likes this man, Nikhil.

Does Vinodini's earnest participation in the group's work indicate that she likes him too?

'Look, this is what your Aunt does – digging empty lakes all over the village too.'

Aphra points to the dark rain clouds.

'Not empty for long.' Says the child.

Lalita inhales deeply.

'See? You can already smell the mud. The most beautiful fragrance in the world.'

'Mum, you are so happy here...'

'I'm happy with those kids at the rehabilitation centre too. And with you.' She tells her daughter.

'And with Dad.' Says Aphra, and Lalita wants to stroke her chin, under it the way her baby used to like, but now the baby has become a little girl. Touches and cuddles are not enough, Aphra needs direct answers to her questions.

The 'and with Dad' is a question.

It is also an order, Lalita owes it to her.

It is also a plea, Lalita's heart aches when she senses that.

Mother and daughter seize the interruption that the sound of an approaching vehicle brings.

And yet, Aphra comes and puts her arm around Lalita's waist and Lalita kisses the top of her child's head.

They stand together and watch Nakusa riding pillion on Jana's scooter.

Jana is now in her late twenties.

She is an M.D.

'So, Nakusa Bai, Jana did get her books,' says Lalita.

'Both are happy that you are trusting them with the hospital,' Jana hugs Lalita.

'We had thought maybe you'd come and stay…' says Jana softly.

'Each of us has a life there. We wanted that inheritance thing to end Jana.'

Jana looks at Lalita.

'So we will always have a gynaecologist and a paediatrician here. And let's see, some other doctors.' Lalita looks at the gate.

'And you have to come often.'

Lalita pats her on her cheek.

There is a clap of thunder. Lalita walks out into the courtyard.

A car approaches. In the hills beyond the road it is already raining. She can hear Raga *Megh* on Santoor.

There is a clap of thunder. It starts raining.

The ground gets covered with water. The trees seem to come to life.

Zaid looks at Lalita. Lalita tries to hide her joy at seeing this man. Zaid runs towards the house holding his bag over his head.

Lalita is totally drenched. Strong, dignified. She looks straight ahead.

***

Baba's car. *It has stopped by the side of the road. A big, dense tree, and then a deep valley – Vinodini, two years old, has stuck her face against the window.*

Mother wipes a fogged glass window. Both are in the backseat of a beautiful black car. Mother has her arm around Vinodini. She points outside the window. It is a bright morning. The road winds along a river. Everything is green and beautiful. Vinodini is trying to see.

'Akka, YOU show me.'

Ten-year-old Lalita, who nobody paid any attention to

until now, comes behind from the front seat, opens the door, brings Vinodini out and points to the bird in the tree: a bird.

'A *Bharadwaj.*'

The bird flies over the valley.

Vinodini is happy. She holds her Akka's hand.

The two sisters start walking uphill.

Lalita and Vinodini walk together alone.

There are some girls who walk alone.

There are some girls who are forced to stand alone.

***

At that temple, one such girl stands on a *paat.*

The child who is being put through some kind of ritual.

A wet frock clings to the child.

She has bundled it and tucked it between her legs. She is repeatedly asked to stand up and sit down.

The child pinches the wet dress away from her chest. The priest holds out a flower and some rice.

To accept those, one of her hands will have to let go of her frock and let the dress stick back to her body.

The wet cloth will cling to her body.

She will feel exposed, watched.

Her eyes search in the smoky dark.

In a corner of the temple, two sisters put their arms around each other.

The girl looks towards the two women.

The End